Coal Blooded

ERNIE BOWLING

PAGE PUBLISHING, INC.
New York, NY

First originally published by Page Publishing, Inc. 2017

ISBN 978-1-64082-873-5 (Paperback)
ISBN 978-1-64082-874-2 (Digital)

Printed in the United States of America

For Karen

"Then there was the whole concept of coal mining, which is a culture unto itself, the most dangerous occupation in the world, and which draws and develops a certain kind of man."
—Martin C. Smith

"Mining is like a search-and-destroy mission."
—Stewart L. Udall

"I still haven't found what I'm looking for."
—U2

Prologue

"Son, have you made any plans?" his father asked.

"Nothing yet, Dad." He hadn't even started looking for work. He was way too busy catching up on his sleep and hanging out with his buddies on the wall until 2:00 a.m., hearing about all the happenings during his months away and on his beer drinking. He was way behind on the beer drinking.

"Well, I have," his father said. "R.T. is waiting to talk with you down at his house. Mosey on down there and talk with him."

R.T. Theodore was the general mine foreman at the coal mine where his father worked. He'd been with the company for almost forty years, transferring from the Itmann mines about the same time as his father. The Theodore house was three doors down, so the walk took only a minute. Mr. Theodore was sitting on his front porch as if he were waiting on the young man.

"How you doing, Mike?" Theodore asked as the young man walked up his steps. "Nice to be back home after your time in the big city?"

"Always good to be home, sir," Mike answered. He was being nice. Actually, he was getting restless at home, and becoming bored. Except for the beer drinking part.

"Given any thought about what you're gonna do now?"

"Hadn't yet," he replied.

"Can use you at the mine, if you're not afraid of hard work."

"No, sir. I'm not afraid of hard work." *I've worked hard in the past*, Mike thought. He has absolutely no idea what hard work was, but he will soon find out.

"Good. Go down to the mine office tomorrow and get your paperwork done up. They'll arrange for your physical. You can start work once that's done."

"Thank you, sir."

"Nah, no need for that. We can always use good men."

Mike stood and shook the old man's hand, then headed for home.

Chapter 1

He perches on his round silver lunch pail, staring at the cold gray elevator doors. It's almost time to go. Soon, the doors will swing open and it will be his turn to enter the dark abyss. His stomach is churning. This isn't what he had planned for his life. His only semester of college he spent partying instead of studying. Now that seems like a long time ago.

The rest of the workmen mill around, joking, checking their cap lights, taking the final drags off the last cigarettes they'll have for eight hours. Most pass by him. A few nod, but none speak to the new guy. He's set apart from the rest of the miners with his shiny new bright red hard hat, stiff new leather miner's belt, and slick rubber boots yet to be covered with the black mud from below. So he sits, deeply breathes the fresh morning mountain air, and stares at the doors. Seven o'clock in the morning comes early. He can't remember when he last was up at this time. Surely, not at college. None of his classes started before ten, and even at that time, he had difficulty getting there.

He hears the sharp click of the motor's contacts, the loud whirr of the hoist engines, and sees the drive drum turning. The cage is coming up. Mr. Theodore has told him this is his trip. The section crews have already gone down on the two earlier trips, and he is to ride on the third trip with the general crew. His heart begins to race. His mouth now bone dry, he spits out the snuff he's been chewing the last half hour. The cage slows as it approaches the landing, and he stands up.

"Ready to go, Mike Thomas?" Mr. Theodore asks as he emerges from the mine office. R.T. Theodore has been the general mine foreman at a Banner Fuels Mine for as long as anyone could remember. His body shows his years in the mines: gravel-voiced, hunchbacked, with hands and face worn and weathered as old leather. He walks with a limp from a mine accident years ago, and he always carries a pick hammer on a three-foot-long handle that doubles as his cane. Since he was a child, Mike has heard stories about the old man: how hard he is on the workers, how he is a dyed-in-the-wool company man, how he doesn't stand for slackers. The mine is his life. Mike's father says you can't talk about the mine without talking about Mr. Theodore. They are one and the same. Mike has known Mr. Theodore since his own family moved to the area when he was just a tyke. Mike has never seen the side of the old man his father and the other workers berate. Theodore and his wife had three girls, the youngest of them—Jenny—Mike's age. They had grown up together, were friends—but nothing more—in high school. She too had gone off to college, but with much better results to show for her first semester. She was still there. Theodore could always be seen at Friday night football games, and Mike could always count on him critiquing his gridiron performance Sunday morning after church. Mike knew nothing of this hard ass his father had warned him about, but now he worried maybe he was about to see that side of the man.

"Reckon I'm as ready as I'm going to be, sir," Mike answers.

"Good. See me when we get off the cage and I'll give you the nickel tour before we work the hell outta you," Theodore says with a hint of a smile.

The steel doors of the cage swing open, and the last of the midnight shift's crews spill off the cage, letting out a loud yell, signaling the end of another safe shift. The men move quickly, almost in a sprint, to the lamp house. Once the cage is cleared, the general crew moves onto the landing. The joking and small talk ceases. Theodore boards last, closes the doors, and rings the bell, signaling the hoist operator to lower the cage. The cage drops slowly at first, gaining speed until it is dropping at what Mike is sure must be near a free-fall. His stomach thinks so anyway. He's sure it's still topside. The bright daylight quickly fades, and everyone almost in unison turns on the battery-powered cap lights attached to their hard hats. The drop down the six-hundred-foot shaft takes less than a minute, and the cage eases slowly to a stop at the bottom. The doors swing open, giving Mike his first view of an underground coal mine.

Mike is speechless at this new world. All the years of hearing his father and uncles talk about the mines never truly described this scene. He steps off the cage and looks at the white— white!—walls of the mine. He touches the wall. The white stuff is moist and thick and sticks to his hand like paste. The tunnel ahead is as straight as an arrow for as far as his cap light will shine. The tunnel is about six feet high and twenty feet wide at best guess and running down the center of the tunnel is a pair of train tracks. Along either side of the tunnel is a row of timbers, so perfectly aligned if you stand in front of one you cannot see the remaining timbers in the row behind, and are fit snugly to the mine roof. Protruding from the roof are square metal plates each with a bolt head in its center, the roof bolts he's heard his dad describe. There are four to a row, and each row lines up almost perfectly with the next, forming four long rows in the roof. To his surprise, there is a strong breeze blowing past him down the entryway, strong enough to move small pieces of trash down the tunnel. Mike stares into the darkness, watching each worker move off into the distance, until all that can be seen of each is the up-and-down bobbing of their cap lights.

"What you expected?" Mr. Theodore asks, observing the new man's first reaction to the underground. He has seen it before countless times.

"Can't say that it is, sir. I know my dad comes home covered in black every day. But all I see here is this thick white stuff."

"The white you see is powdered limestone we call rock dust. It starts out dry, but the moisture in the mine air causes it to thicken and cake. We use it everywhere. It covers the coal dust to prevent it from catching fire if we ever have an explosion. Most of the outlying areas, where you'll be for the next six months, are covered with it. Up on the sections where the coal is mined, we use it too, but the coal dust is much thicker there. That coal dust is what your daddy wears home. Come on, I'll show you around."

For the next two hours Mike walks around the mine with Theodore, listening as the old man explains how the mine operates.

Theodore reaches into the breast pocket of his coveralls and pulls out a worn map of the mine and, unfolding it, shows it to Mike. It looks like an underground city! The mine is a series of long, continuous tunnels with connecting cross tunnels, or crosscuts, spaced at preset distances determined by the mine engineers. These intersecting tunnels leave huge blocks of coal, or pillars, between them to support the mine roof. The mine is ever expanding in all directions as the coal is removed from its bed or seam. The areas where the coal is being extracted are called sections, and the Banner Fuels Mine currently has five working sections, each over a mile from one another. Each section operates in a direction of the compass—north, south, east, and west—and the fifth section works on retreat mining, or "pulling pillars" as Theodore calls it. This is the area where only the most experienced miners work, as the roof can, and does, cave in at any moment. This is where Mike's father works. The number of operating sections varies from time to time depending on working conditions, coal orders, and the company's business plans. He listens intently as Theodore explains mine ventilation, how the air is brought into the mine by a series of large ventilating fans located on the surface. The air is directed through the mine to its final destination, the working sections, by means of barricades in the crosscuts, which prevent the air from escaping the mine too early. The air must reach the working face, or actual area where the coal is being mined, to provide fresh air to the workmen and carry away the dangerous methane gas liberated in the mining process. The methane is really what's dangerous, Theodore explains. It is colorless, odorless, tasteless, and highly explosive. It can explode in as low as a 5 percent concentration, but the fresh air blowing through the mine usually keeps the concentration from ever nearing that point. Mike doesn't understand anything the old man is saying, but it is interesting, and he tries to show the boss his attentiveness. As he walks and talks, Theodore often stops to pick up a piece of trash, reset a dislodged timber, rehang a sagging power or communications cable attached to the timbers along the walls of the tunnel, or entry in miner's slang. Mike tries to pitch in and help as best he can. Mike will get to see the section someday, Theodore promises, but the mine laws state that novice coal miners must first work in the outlying, or outby, areas doing support work: setting timbers, spreading rock dust, taking supplies to the sections, advancing the conveyor belts that carry the mined coal to the central coal bin at the bottom of the mine shaft, where it is then carried to the surface by yet another large conveyor belt. But first, Mike will learn the most basic of mine jobs—shoveling coal.

Theodore holds open a small square metal door and Mike bends over and steps through. He sees a long rubber conveyor belt resting in a cradle of three rollers shaped in a "V" that loudly hum as they turn. These belts literally run for miles. The conveyor is covered with coal so continuous and even that it gives the conveyor the appearance of a rapidly moving black river. The coal spills from the belts regularly, and someone has to shovel the coal back onto the belts, for if too large a spill is allowed to accumulate, a fire can occur from the friction of the conveyor running through the loose coal. That someone, Theodore informs Mike, is going to be him for the next few months. Mike notices a cap light bobbing in the distance, getting larger as the worker approaches the two men. It is the belt foreman, who Theodore explains has the responsibility of keeping the conveyors running smoothly. If the conveyors stop, coal production stops, and that is totally unacceptable. There is a crew of twenty men assigned to the conveyors, and the foreman is responsible for keeping them busy.

"Mr. Riggs, meet Mr. Thomas. He's all yours now." And with that short introduction, Theodore disappears into the darkness, leaving the two miners alone.

"Come with me," the foreman says matter-of-factly. The two walk the belt line for a short distance without sharing any words. Soon, they come upon another miner kneeling at the side of the conveyor belt, shovel in hand. Mike can see this is a very old workman, who struggles to raise himself and greet the two. He's got on a pair of kneepads. Why, Mike wonders, is this fella wearing kneepads? He's heard his dad talk of the need for them in the low coal seams, but in here, it's six feet high.

"Howdy, boss!" the old man yells. "See ya got the redcap with ya!" Mike isn't sure if the raised voice is due to the loud beltline or if the geezer has a hearing problem.

"How's it goin', Lacey?" the foreman asks, not really expecting or wanting an answer. "The kid will be with you the rest of the shift. Take care of him, will ya?" the boss asks, although it sounds more like a command than a question. "I've got a belt move to get done on two sections. You make your way to the bottom at shift's end. Show him the ropes. Don't get him hurt." That last statement gives Mike a bit of a scare. Riggs grabs a large coal shovel resting against the mine wall and tosses the shovel to Mike. "This is all you'll be needin' for a while. Keep up with it," the boss orders. "Now, y'all get busy. I'm gone!" Mike and the old miner watch as the belt foreman moves quickly up the belt line until he too is lost in the darkness.

"Well, come on, young'un, we've got a mile of belt to clean!" the old man yells as he drops back onto his knees and begins to shovel from under the moving belt. For the next six hours, the two men shovel spilled coal back onto the conveyor belt. Mike tries bending over to shovel the coal, but his back quickly begins to ache, and before long, he is breathing hard and sweating profusely. There is no breeze on the belt line as there was on the track. He's trying hard to keep up with the old man, who's down on his knees, shoveling steadily and leaving Mike in the dust. So he tries kneeling. It is easier to work in this position, Mike thinks, but damn, if it ain't hard on the knees. The knees! That's why the old guy is wearing the pads. It's easier on the knees. But Mike plugs along, albeit at a much slower pace than the old hand. He nearly loses his shovel several times to the rapidly moving conveyor. He isn't used to this kind of labor. The only job he'd previously had was pumping gas at a buddy's gas station. Check the tires, pump the gas, and flirt with the girls. Pretty cushy compared to where he was now. Besides his back, his knees also ache, his hands are sore, his pants are soaked from the wet coal and rock dust he's kneeling in, and his shirt is so saturated from his sweat it sticks to him like a second skin. And there is no end of the belt line in sight. He and Lacey, separated by the belt and the noise, rarely speak throughout the day, so Mike is left with his work and his thoughts. His main thought: I'm exhausted and I'm miserable. Only six hundred feet below ground, but this must be close to hell.

Not soon enough Lacey stops his shoveling and the two miners start the long walk toward the mineshaft. As they near the bottom, Mike sees a group of men approaching. Can't be the next shift, he thinks. It's too early for them. He counts six—no, seven. They walk up to Mike, stopping him in his tracks. Lacey walks on. He recognizes several of the men, all from one of the sections. Must've missed their trip. The biggest one of the bunch sticks out his hand and says, "Welcome to the big mine." Mike grabs his hand to shake, when suddenly the other men jump him and wrestle him to the ground. While four of them hold Mike down, the fifth undoes his miner's belt and pants, jerking them down to Mike's knees. He struggles. He isn't a small guy, but he is no match for all of them. A sixth miner brings in a large metal bucket full of bearing grease and proceeds to cover Mike's gonads with a heavy layer of the goo. A seventh miner tosses several handfuls of rock dust on top of the grease, as another removes Mike's hard hat and gives his head a dose of the same mixture. It's over in less than a minute. The men all laugh heartily, and Mike, once over the shock of the ordeal, tries to do the same. Greasing the new guy is a mine tradition. His father had told him it was coming, and how well a new hire takes goes a long way toward being accepted by the miners. It wasn't as bad as the hazing he'd taken when he pledged the college fraternity. The men help him up from the ground and hold his miner's belt and cap as he dresses. There are slaps on the back, and much joking at Mike's expense occurs on the cage ride to the surface and, again, by the evening shift crews as Mike passes them into the bathhouse. His father gives him a quick once-over on the way onto the cage, making sure he's none the worse for wear. Even Mr. Theodore makes a rare trip out of the mine office to survey the damage done to his new hire. Mike's dirty, he's tired, but he's proud of himself. He has survived his first day in the mine.

Chapter 2

The Banner Fuels Mine is large. It is also very old. The mine covers several square miles of underground area. The mine is also unique in that it is one of a few mines that actually work two coal seams simultaneously. Due to the mountain geology, two coal seams lie close to one another. The Pocahontas 3 seam lies at a depth of six hundred feet below the surface. This seam is very high, over thirteen feet in some areas, and this seam was the source of the initial growth in the region. The area's nickname, "The Pocahontas Coal Fields," comes from the early mining of this coal seam. The Pocahontas 3 seam is the seam mined by most of the large coal companies in the area: US Steel, Keystone Fuels, Consolidated Coal Company. This seam has been continuously worked for over a hundred years in the mountains of southern West Virginia and southwest Virginia, and it is rapidly playing out.

Fortunately, about eighty feet above the 3 seam lies the Pocahontas 4 seam. Considerably thinner, only four to six feet in height, this seam had been ignored by the large coal companies who chose to focus their efforts on the thicker 3 seam, but with depleting reserves of the larger seam, the companies have turned their attention to the 4 seam. Banner Fuels is no different. The mining companies also own the mineral rights to the 4 seam, but attacking this seam presents its own unique challenges. The larger equipment used in the 3 seam won't fit in the 4 seam. Mining equipment is designed and manufactured for the seam height, and the larger equipment designed for the 3 seam is too large for the smaller seam. The mining machines would have to cut too much rock for clearance, which would create problems in the preparation plant separating the rock from the coal, thus increasing the cost per ton mined, so most coal companies have chosen to completely exhaust their 3 seam reserves, scrap their large equipment, then re-tool and start over with smaller equipment in the upper thinner seam.

Banner Fuels has chosen a different approach. The company cut an inclined slope from the lower seam to the upper seam, 250 feet long on a thirty-degree pitch, and began mining the coal out of the 4 seam over already mined out areas of the 3 seam below. The company ran track up the slope for coal car haulage, blasting out enough overhead clearance for the large coal cars, then installed a conveyor belt haulage system to deliver coal from the section to the coal cars. The conveyor belt system also serves as a supply system to the lone 4 seam section. The track haulage delivers coal off the section and supplies to the belt header. The conveyor belt, when running forward, delivers the coal from the section to the cars. The section supplies are loaded onto the belt at the header by the motormen, and with the belt running in reverse, the supplies are "back belted" to the belt tail piece, where they are offloaded by the section crew. This is a slow, cumbersome, yet necessary evil as the track motors and cars are likewise too tall to operate in the lower seam. The workmen, the supplies, and the only means of ingress and egress to the 4 seam section is by belt, or crawling on your hands and knees for two miles from the belt head to the working section.

Mike has shoveled this 4 seam belt, as he has shoveled all the belts on 3 seam in the two months since his hire. He spends his time shoveling on his knees wherever he is. The only difference as far as he's concerned between the two seams is he can't stand and stretch his aching back when he shovels the 4 seam belt. Days run together on the belt crew. The scenery is unchanging: just miles upon seemingly endless miles of conveyor belt as far as the eye can see and the cap light can shine.

Working in the mines isn't without its benefits. One morning, Mike pulls his new Mustang into the bathhouse parking lot. Usually full of beat-up old Fords and Chevy trucks, today the lot is half-empty. Gathering his lunch pail, he walks up to a group of miners gathered around a fire ablaze in an oil drum, attempting to take the chill off the early-morning mountain air.

"What's up, fellas?" Mike asks to no one in particular.

"Mine's down today, rook," one miner answers. Mike recognizes him as one of the section men, but doesn't know his name. "Mine fatality."

Mine fatality. Mike has heard this term his entire life, the first time as a young child. A generic term for a man killed underground. For some reason, he thought that was the term used by folks outside the mine. He never figured the men underground used it as well. He'd always thought the miners were more descriptive of what had happened, like a code or something. He was surprised to learn otherwise. A fatality wasn't something he'd thought much about since he started working underground. You think about it too much and you'll drive yourself crazy. Or get hurt yourself. He's only been here a few months, and this is this first time someone's been killed underground in—well, he can't recall the last fatality.

"What happened?" he asks meekly. He doesn't know these men, he's the new guy, and he doesn't know how to broach the subject.

"Belt man," another miner answers. Mike feels his stomach come up into his throat.

"Man fell into the drive unit of the conveyor belt at the 4 seam header," the miner continues, all the while gazing into the fire. "The roller drums crushed him. Mashed him to a pulp."

"How could that happen?" Mike blurts out. The conveyor drive unit is housed in a chain-link fence enclosure as required by federal law, and besides, the design of the conveyor belt drive unit would carry a body away from the drive unit if the belt were hauling coal.

"Well, that's the big question," another miner answers, loading his jaw with chewing tobacco. "They were back-belting roof bolts and rock dust to the section. The header man was loading the supplies, and the crew was off-loading them at the feeder. The last of the supplies were off, and the crew had called to the header to switch the belt back around to forward so they could load coal. But he never answered. They didn't know anything was wrong until they saw blood and guts coming up the bottom belt. The boss then crawled out to the header. I heard the only thing left was the man's lower legs from his knees to his boots hanging out from the drive unit."

"What gets me," another miner interjects, "is what in the hell was the guy doing in there in the first place? Shit, he had to take down the chain-link fence to get in there. And there was no reason for him to be in there anyway. Damn peculiar if you ask me."

"You damn skippy, hoss," the first miner adds. "Of all the ways down there to go, that ain't one of the ways you'd think of. Heard they've got a crew of men scattering rock dust for the length of the belt, trying to cover up the blood, guts, and shit."

Shaken, Mike walks into the bathhouse. A few men are milling around quietly, gathering their work clothes. Peering through the bathhouse doors into the lamp house, Mike observes a beehive of activity. Federal mine inspectors in their trademark reflective striped coveralls are everywhere, looking at maps, reviewing record books, and talking to the 4 seam crew and section foreman. Mr. Theodore goes from one group to the next, listening intently, offering comment when asked. Mike is so focused on the scene before him he jumps when he feels a hand on his shoulder.

"Go on home, young'un," Cal Ripley, one of the section foremen, says to him, a look of sorrow on his face. "Nothin' for you to do here. We may get back at it tomorrow."

Mike silently nods. He really doesn't want to be here right now. He leaves without talking to anyone and slowly eases his Mustang off the mine property.

Chapter 3

The mine quickly returns to normal. Rumors about the fatality abound. A coal mine generates as much gossip as it does coal. The first rumor to surface said the workman was deeply in debt and committed suicide by leaping into the drive unit. A second quickly followed that he was having an affair with the wife of a coworker who ambushed him and threw him into the machinery. Mike never hears the official version rendered by the enforcement agencies. That wouldn't be as juicy to the miners anyway.

For the next four months, Mike toils away in the bowels of the earth, learning more tricks of the mining trade. He learns to install conveyor belts, how to align them so they would spill less coal, which was a very valuable little lesson, saving Mike many a backache.

He learns how to set timbers and build cribs. He learns how to install track, how to set a pump, how to lay block—all skills he'd never be exposed to topside, skills unique to the mine that have no real use above ground. He was growing in confidence and no longer worried about the mountain of rock over his head. He quit worrying if the mountain was going to fall on him as he did incessantly the first few weeks on the job. But mainly he shovels. A lot. Eight hours a day, five days a week, for months. Initially, he was so tired he would fall asleep at the dinner table. He developed muscles he didn't know he had, and he had been a dedicated weightlifter in high school. He didn't spend much time hanging out with his buddies, as his evenings were spent in bed, utterly exhausted from the day's work and resting for the day to come.

He's been a steady worker and hasn't missed a shift since he started. He's lucky he's been able to stay on the day shift this long.

Most new trainees are rolled to the evening or midnight shift as soon as the union begins moaning to management. All hourly employees at the mine, underground or surface, are contracted members of the United Mine Workers Association or UMWA. All job openings are supposed to be placed open for bid. All union employees are eligible to bid on any open jobs, with the winning bidder selected by seniority, or time of service at the mine. It is in this manner an employee can move to another shift, or another job, if he can prove he can perform the job requirements. General labor, the kind Mike has been performing, is a job any miner can do, and day shift jobs are the goal of most miners. The union leaders feel Mike's general labor job should be posted for bidding so a more senior man can move to the day shift, but Mr. Theodore stubbornly refuses. Mike is a trainee, he argues, and trainee jobs are not subject to bid. The union leaders can't argue, for they know the old boss is correct. Mr. Theodore has never cared for the union, but he knows their contract inside and out. He knows what he can and can't do and pushes that envelope at every available opportunity. The union will get just what their contract outlines and nothing more. Mike will move to a different shift once he gets rid of the red cap.

Mike wants to move to another shift. The miners on the first shift have all been at the mine for many years, married and with families, and are interested in putting in their day's work and heading home in the evenings. Most of the miners Mike's age work on the midnight shift or "hoot owl" shift as it's referred to at the mine. His buddies gather in the mornings after the shift is over at one of the local watering holes to drink beer and talk trash. Some days, while he is shoveling the conveyor belts, Mike thinks about his buddies out partying while he slaves away with old man Lacey. It helps to pass the time. When Mike finishes his shift, his friends are home sleeping. The first few weeks, until he adjusted to the hard physical demands of his job, he spent every free moment sleeping. Now that he's grown accustomed to the work, he has time for prowling, but to no avail. There is no one out and about in the evening, so Mike is left to wander the streets. He drives around the small town for hours in his new car, the down payment made with his first paycheck. He stops at the two local drive-ins, carrying on conversations with the car-hops and anyone who'll stop and talk. The first few months he's content, as he catches everyone up on the recent happenings in his life— his new job, his new car, and his work at the mine. But for the most part, his social life is nonexistent.

Mike has learned a lot about the mine in his months on the job. He's also grown stronger and put on a few pounds of muscle. Eating well has helped. His mom always was a good cook, and she feeds her only boy well. And the money's good. More money than he ever earned working the penny-anty job he held in high school. Still, his first paycheck was a shock. The withholdings, some he'd never even heard of before, was a chunk of money, and the union also takes their cut of his pay for union dues. Still, he was able to buy his first car, a brand-new cherry-red Mustang with a 359 cubic-inch engine, four-on-the-floor, a jam-up stereo system with an AM/FM radio, and one of those new eight-track tape players. He's got all the hot tapes to play—Boston, The Eagles, James Taylor, Elton John.

Since no one is around after his shift, Mike spends most of his afternoons driving around, playing his stereo really loud, drinking a few beers. One afternoon, he's barreling along the highway and passes Theodore's house. He's done this a thousand times since coming home, but on this day, he sees Jennifer Theodore sitting on the front porch. He almost breaks his neck looking around for a second glance, to make sure it's her. He locks up the car's brakes, does a fishtail in the middle of the highway, and flies the Mustang into her driveway.

Jennifer has a stunned look on her face, as if thinking, "Who's this idiot in the hot-rod?" until Mike steps out of the car.

"Hey, Jennifer. How's it going?" Mike says with a wide smile as he bounds up the six steps in two large strides. "Haven't seen you since graduation."

"I'm great, Mike," she replies as she greets him with a big hug. "It's really good to see you. Dad told me you're working at the mine. How do you like it?"

"Ah, it's a living, I guess. Seemed I was all out of options after college didn't work out. Anyway, the work's hard, but the money's good."

"That I see," she said, pointing her head at the shiny new car. "Had that long?"

"Nah. A few months. Ain't she a beaut?" he says with obvious pride. "And she'll run like a scalded dog. Wanna go for a ride?"

"I'd love to, but, please, none of the stuff you pulled getting in here!" Jennifer sticks her head in the front door, tells her mom she's going out, and piles into the front seat. Mike shuts the door behind her (*I'd better be a gentleman to the boss's daughter*, he figures), and the two take to the road and start to catch up.

"So, Jen, how long you been home?"

"About two months. I'm heading back soon. Classes start after Labor Day."

"First year at WVU go okay?" he asks.

"Yes. It was harder than I expected. Getting around was a pain. The winter was really cold, even colder than here. And I got homesick, so getting back was a welcome relief. How about you, Mike? I heard you only stayed at school one semester. What happened?"

"So many parties, so little time," he half-heartedly jokes. "My mom says I didn't make good use of my time. My dad says I wasn't disciplined enough. I think I was just enjoying being away from home too much. Either way, the grades went down the tubes, and the money was gone. So I had to come home."

"Well, are you going back?"

"Can't afford it right now. College ain't cheap, and my folks ain't paying for it. If I do go back, I'll be on my dime. Besides, I really don't know what I'd study if I did go back."

"I thought you wanted to be a coach."

"Fat chance of that happening. I reckon my semester in college put an end to that plan."

"Mike, there's always hope. You can't get down on yourself because of one bad turn. It's like my dad says: life's a marathon race and we've just started running. Slow and steady wins the race. Besides, you're a pretty sharp guy. You didn't do well in college because you were too busy doing other things besides studying, not because you lack the intelligence. If you applied yourself, I'm sure you'd succeed."

"Now you're starting to sound like my mother. For now, to hell with it. Wanna get something to eat?" he asks as he pulls into one of the stalls at the drive-in. The conversation turns to small talk as the two make a meal on cheeseburgers, french fries, and beer. The two drive around the town for another hour, when Mike realizes it's getting late and turns the car for home. Theodore is waiting on the porch when he pulls into the driveway. Again he gets out first and opens her car door. The whole time, though, his eyes are on his boss.

"Nice to see you getting my daughter home at a decent hour, Mister Thomas," Theodore says with a half-sharp tone to his voice that Mike doesn't recognize... or like. Mike looks at his watch - 9 pm. Not late, but 7 am comes early for him. Theodore is well known to be at the mine by 5 am. Mike is surprised he's still up.

"Well, sir, I've got to be up early tomorrow, as you know." Mike says a little sheepishly. He doesn't want to raise the old man's ire.

"Yeah, I know getting up early is tough. But you don't have to worry about it much longer," the old man says while rocking in the wicker chair. "Your six-month training period is over this Friday. I can't keep you on day shift any longer than that. The union leaders will bitch to high heaven if I do. So, next week, you start on the evening shift."

Evening shift? The words hit Mike like a ton of bricks. He assumed he'd be heading to the midnight shift with his buddies, where all the new hires eventually wind up. The shock and disappointment are evident on his face. Theodore sees it. So does Jennifer. Stunned, he blurts out the question, "Why?" without thinking of whom he's asking.

"Because it's where you're needed," Theodore answers sharply. He isn't used to having his decisions questioned. But then again, the employee's immediate foreman usually delivers this news to the new hires. Mike immediately regains his composure. He dares not question the big boss again. Theodore's word is law at the mine. It won't do any good to request a shift change through the union. It isn't a seniority issue. Management can put him wherever they damn well please. The only way off evening shift now is to bid off, or leave. And he damn sure isn't leaving.

"You'll be working for David Hatfield on Number Four section. Do a good job," Theodore adds as he disappears into the house, leaving Mike and Jennifer alone on the porch. *A section! I'm going to get to work on a section! Maybe this won't be so bad, after all,* he thinks. Most of his friends on the midnight shift are doing support work—rock dusting the belt lines, hauling supplies, repairing track, setting timbers. None of them are regularly working on a section. Everyone in the mine knows a section is the place to be if you want to make money. It's where the highest-paying jobs are. It's where the coal is actually being mined, and that is what pays the way for the company. Many days the section crews work overtime if they've got a good production run going. And it's where the danger is as well. After all, the high-paying jobs all come with more risk. Most of the accidents in the mine happen on the working sections. The danger aspect stokes Mike's macho blood a bit.

The sudden work news and Mike's subsequent facial expressions have been on full view for Jennifer. First the shock, then bewilderment, and finally the subtle smile that came on his face has amused her. He was always easy to read, she thinks, or at least she always could read him. Like a book.

"Well, you OK?" she asks. "Need to sit down? Need a drink? What?"

"No, I'm OK," he replies. "Guess I'd better get home. Day shift comes early, but as your dad said, I don't have to worry about it for long."

"You all right with the evening shift?" she asks. The concerned look on her face touches him.

"Yeah, might as well be. Nothing to be done about it anyway. Once you're there, you're there. The hours suck. Three to 11:00 p.m. Look like I'll be living for the weekends, that's for sure. But at least I'll be on a section, learning to run the equipment and such. Dad says it's important to be able to operate all the equipment. It will make you more able to bid up if you want. Hey, since this is my last Friday night free for a while, you wanna go see what's playing at the Pocahontas theatre?" Mike knows this means giving up his Friday evening drinking beer with his buddies, but thinks he might be able to catch up with them after he drops her home.

"Sure, Mike, sounds like fun. Pick me up at six thirty. The movie always starts at seven."

"Sounds like a plan to me. See you then, Jen," he says, jumping in and firing up the Mustang. Jennifer watches as he drives down the highway, tossing her a wave as he heads home. Passing through her living room, her father, now situated comfortably in his recliner, asks her to sit with him for a moment. She rests on the arm of the chair and puts her arm around her father's neck.

"Well, how'd he take the news?"

"He's fine, Daddy," Jennifer answers. "He seemed a little disappointed to be going to the evening shift. I think he expected to go to the midnight shift with the rest of his friends."

"No, that's not for him," Theodore explains. "Those guys on the owl shift ain't worth killin'. Bunch of drugged-out crazies if you ask me. Why, in a year's time won't any of 'em be left. They'll all be fired for missing too much work or have quit. There's good men on the evening shift. Steady men. Family men. The crew he's going to be with is the best on that shift. Wildcat Hatfield is as fine a boss as I have. Mike will learn from them. Besides, if he takes the superintendent's offer, he won't have time for farting around anyway."

"What offer is that, Daddy?" Jennifer asks.

"Well, it ain't my place to say right now, darlin'. And don't you go sayin' anything to him about none of this neither. Well, it's past my bedtime, honey. I'm off to the sack." The old man rises slowly, kisses his youngest daughter on the forehead, and makes his way upstairs to bed.

Chapter 4

Mike's last day shift is uneventful. He delivered some machine parts with the supply crew to several sections, helped lay a track turnout, and with Lacey, the last half of the shift he shoveled the belt line and reset loose timbers along the belt. Mike is more than a little apprehensive as he approaches shaft bottom at the end of the shift. These guys don't pass up any opportunity to grease someone, and his rolling off the shift might be a good-enough reason for them. The only occurrence out of the ordinary is when Mike's boss tells him to take the first trip up. He always rides the last cage to the surface, but he doesn't place any significance to this early escape. As the cage slows to the landing, Mike sees his father waiting for his trip down. Usually, by the time Mike's trio reaches the surface, his father's crew is on the way to their section.

Mike's father has worked for years on the evening shift as a continuous miner operator. It is the highest-paying union job in the mine. He won't be working on his father's section, and for that, Mike is thankful. The experience might prove to be uncomfortable for them both. He and his father have never been close, what with him working the evening shift while Mike was in school. The only time they ever spent together was on weekends. Even then, they never connected. Mike could never recall his father doing any of the activities most men did, like hunting, fishing, or bowling. Just work and watch television. What a life. The two of them had begun communicating after Mike started working in the mine. His dad would ask how his week had gone, what was he doing, while Mike would ask questions about the section, about actually mining coal, the mine gossip, and general mining questions. After eighteen years, they finally had something in common: work. Damn. The distance between them seemed to be dissipating, then came the conversation on the front porch the Sunday after Mike got his first paycheck.

"Get your first payday Friday, son?" his father asked.

"Damn sure did. More money than I've ever had in my life," Mike answered with pride.

"Reckon that's enough for you to now get a place of your own?"

Mike thought about the question. He could get mad. He could be hurt that his father was putting him out. But his father had a wife and a daughter and a mortgage. Mike had none of these and was making damn near the money his dad was making.

"Reckon so, Dad."

He moved into his apartment the next week.

"Hey, Dad, not used to seeing you topside," Mike says to his father.

"I see they let you up early today," his father replies. "I reckon they're letting you slide on your last day. Let's you and I go over here a minute. There's someone you need to meet." The two men walk over to a group of ten miners huddled around an oil drum. "Hey, Wildcat, want ya to meet my son. Boy, this here's Mr. Hatfield. You're gonna be working for him."

David Hatfield is a mountain of a man. Mike figures him to be six feet four easy, three hundred pounds if he is an ounce. He was said to have descended from the original Hatfields of the legendary mountain feud. He looked like one of those Russian weightlifters and was about his dad's age, around forty. His face covered with a thick, long beard that hasn't seen a razor in years. His father said the beard covers some scars he acquired in a scrap with a mountain cat he'd captured trapping years ago, hence, the nickname. He looks down at Mike, sizing him up.

"Ready to come to a good section, boy?" Wildcat asks in a deep, thunderous voice as big as the man. Mike is at once impressed and intimidated. He reminds him of his high-school football coach. The man commands respect, like Theodore.

"Yes, sir!" Mike replies as he stands up straight, almost coming to attention before catching himself. The other miners in the group snicker at the youngster's actions.

"Good. Keep your eyes open and your mouth shut and I'll make a damn coal miner out of you," the foreman bellows. "Good-lookin' boy you got there, Thomas. See he gets some rest Sunday. We'll work the shit out of him Monday," he adds just before jumping on the cage.

"Damn, what a big man," Mike says to his father as the cage disappears from view.

"Yeah, big enough to not take any crap off anybody," his father adds. "But he's a fair man. You could do worse for a boss. Anyway, my trip is next and there's something I want to give you. You're not a trainee anymore. The red cap comes off next shift. I thought you might like a different hard hat than the one you're wearing." His father shoves a brown paper bag into Mike's hands.

Mike reaches into the bag and withdraws a shiny black hard hat. Not just any hard hat, but an old-style cap called a low-vein hat. The new hats, like he's been wearing since he started work, sit very high on the head and have a raised appearance. These old-style hats sit low on the head, like a baseball cap, and are thought to be more comfortable. They're not manufactured anymore, yet are still legal to wear underground, and most are very old, very rare, and very valuable. Miners have been known to offer a hundred dollars or more for a useable low-vein hard hat. Someone has done some work on this cap to make it look shiny new.

"Where'd you get this, Dad?" Mike asks excitedly. This is almost as cool as getting his car. It's the first gift he can recall ever receiving from his father.

"I've had it for years," his father replies, smiling. His son's excitement brings him joy, knowing he gave his boy something he likes and can use. "Always thought I ought to have a spare, in case anything ever happened to mine. Figured you might like to have it."

"Looks like a new one."

"Nah, I just refinished it. Amazin' what a little sandpaper and paint can accomplish, with a little fiberglass sealer to fill in the cracks. Put on a few stickers and it'll look real good."

"Thanks, Dad," Mike says to his father. Knowing his father actually put time into repairing the cap for him makes it even more special. He shakes his father's hand and watches him board his trip and disappear into the black hole. As he hangs up his cap light in the lamp room, Theodore yells from his office for him to come see him before he leaves. Mike is a little leery. Being called into the foreman's room is like going to the school principal's office. You don't know why you've been called, but it usually isn't good. Theodore is sitting behind his metal desk, a gosh-awful puke green color that has been stained over the years with grease, oil, coal dust, tobacco juice, and spilled coffee. His roller chair is the same dingy green, and the seat is totally black from years of ground-in coal dirt. Theodore gazes at Mike over the top of his black horned-rim reading glasses as he studies the day's production reports. Mike gazes at the mine maps covering the office walls like wallpaper, waiting for the old man to speak.

"The super wants to see you down at the big office at three thirty. Better shower quick. He don't like to be kept waiting," Theodore says, never looking up from the pages before him. "Well, that's all. Get going."

The superintendent wants to see me? What the hell for? Mike wonders as he quickly bathes and dresses. He's never met the man. Wouldn't know him if he jumped up and bit him on the ass. Mike has only been to the main mine office twice, first to fill out a job application and then to sign all the employment paperwork a few days later. Both times he was barely in the front door. He drives his Mustang down the mountainside the mile or so to the mine office. The mine office and coal preparation plant are located in a wide spot at the base of the mountain along the railroad tracks. The coal exits the mine carried by a long conveyor belt up a half-mile long slope before it is dumped into the preparation plant, where the coal is washed, sized, and loaded into coal cars to be delivered to the customers thousands of miles away. The mine office is where all the business activities of the mine occur. The superintendent is the one man responsible for the entire operation at the mine, at least on paper. Theodore runs the underground while the superintendent handles everything else. He rarely ever goes underground, and when he does, it usually makes for big news on the underground telephones and two-way radios. The current superintendent, Mr. Stone, is a transplanted Pennsylvanian sent down by the parent company to run things. He'd been at the mine for three or four years now, as best Mike can recall. He has a daughter that was several years ahead of Mike in high school, but was now at some high-priced college up north. Mike made his way into the building and upstairs to the super's office. Unlike the foreman's office up the hill at the mine portal, the super's office is very clean, organized, and businesslike with a receptionist to greet him in the waiting area. It reminds Mike of a doctor's office. While waiting, Mike looks at the photos on the wall and mementos scattered around the bookshelves: golf balls, plaques, awards, the mining engineering diploma from West Virginia University. The super comes in a side door, introduces himself, and asks Mike to sit down. Mike slides deep into a high-backed chair while the super occupies his chair behind an enormous desk. Mike notices that the chair he's in is quite a bit lower to the ground than the super's, forcing him to look up at the super to make eye contact. If he was feeling uneasy before, this positioning definitely makes it worse. He wonders if it is deliberate.

"Mr. Thomas," the superintendent begins, "you come from good stock. Your dad has been with the company for twenty-five years, and your uncle longer than that. Both are good, steady workmen with excellent records and have never caused one minute's trouble. I've noticed that you haven't missed a day's work in your short time here either. I can tell from your high school grades that you are also a bright young man. So I want to know something now that you've been here six months. It is in your blood? Do you have a desire to be a professional coal miner? Or is this going to be just a job to you?"

The question catches Mike off guard. He wasn't sure what to expect here, and a discussion about his future wasn't anywhere on his list. Mike squirms in the chair. "Well, sir, I can't say I've given it much thought," he honestly replies.

"It's about time to give your future some thought, young man," he adds. The words cut through to Mike's soul like a sharp blade. He's heard these words from his parents a hundred times over, but never with the intensity of this moment. The super leans forward and places his elbows on the desk. "Coal mining is changing. The pick-and-shovel days are gone. Each section underground has over a million dollars of highly specialized equipment, and coal miners are some of the highest hourly wage earners on earth. The time has come where we need highly trained supervisors to handle all of this. Don't get me wrong. In my book, experience is still the best teacher. But now it takes more than that to be successful. You got to have a head on your shoulders to boot.

"You've made quite an impression on Mr. Theodore. He thinks you have what it takes to be a company man. Is he right?"

"I haven't given it too much thought, sir," Mike says sheepishly, grinding his butt even deeper into the chair. He feels like he's attending a revival service, so strong are the convictions in the man's voice.

"Well, I hope he is. So here's what we want you to think about. We'd like you to study mining engineering. You can take the first two years of study at the local college, the prerequisites and such, in the mornings before your shift starts. If you do well, you can transfer to Virginia Tech or WVU and co-op your last two years. When you're done, they'll be a management job here for you."

"I can't afford college right now, sir," Mike adds, looking down at the floor. If he could afford college, he'd still be there.

"We're not asking you to do this all on your own," Stone replies. "We'll totally reimburse you for tuition and books, providing you make and keep a B average." Mike figures he must've heard about his semester at college. Gee, this guy does his homework. "So I've given you a lot to think about. Get on outta here and enjoy your weekend."

"Thank you for your time, sir," Mike says politely as he shakes the super's hand and exits the office. His head is spinning. He mentally replays the conversation several times on the drive home. He is so preoccupied he almost forgets he has a date this evening. He hurriedly changes into more appropriate attire, which for him means clean blue jeans and a button down shirt, throws on some cologne, and heads to Jennifer's house. He parks his car in his parents' driveway, as he doesn't want anyone to see his car parked at the Theodore house. It's a little early, but he hopes to catch the old man at home.

He isn't disappointed. Theodore is sitting in his front porch rocker. Mike parks himself on the top step.

"My daughter's inside. Go on in, Thomas," Theodore invites. But Mike hesitates. He has some things on his mind.

"In a minute, sir. Can I talk to you for just a moment?"

"Sure, Mike. What's on your mind?" the old man asks, never ceasing the back and forth of the rocker.

"The conversation I had with Mr. Stone. I'm assuming you had something to do with that whole thing."

"Well, yes, but only a little. The parent company sent a memo to all the mines a few months ago, asking to identify future talent for mining careers. I told 'em I thought you'd be a good candidate, that's all. Was that the subject of your talk with Stone?" the boss asks with a sly smile.

"You know good and well it was," Mike replies. "Look, I appreciate all you've done to help me these last few months. I'm beholdin' to ya. But I ain't sure this is what I want to do for the rest of my life."

"Well, ain't nobody holdin' a gun to your head. Just thought it would be a good opportunity for you. There's enough coal in my mine to last for the next fifty years. Long enough for your working life. Coal mining has been very good to me. I'm sure if you ask your daddy, he'll tell you the same. It's hard work, but honest work. At least you wouldn't be wearing a suit all day, stuck in some office returning phone calls and counting beans for a living. Never trust a man who wears a tie, son," Theodore offers, all the while rocking steadily in his chair. "And it ain't like you got to make a decision today. Just wanted to give you an option, that's all."

Mike feels better after hearing Theodore. *I don't have to decide anything today. Yea, that's it*, he thinks. *Take some time to digest all of this. Put it off awhile. I'll think about it tomorrow. Tonight, Jen and I are going out.*

The young lady emerges from the house as her father is finishing his comments. Her shoulder-length brown hair has been fixed by someone in town, and her cheeks and lips radiate in the evening light. She is wearing a flowery summer dress, and Mike has never seen her dressed in this fashion. She looks really pretty, like someone in those women's magazines his mother keeps in the bathroom. Mike is floored. "Damn, you clean up good, girl," Mike kids as they walk to his parked car three doors up in his parents' driveway. His mother comes out to say hello before the two drive off. This is as close as Mike has ever come to bringing a girl home to meet his mother, and Mrs. Thomas isn't going to let the occasion pass, even if she has known Jennifer since she was a child. The two young people head toward town, with Mike taking it very easy on the accelerator as both parents are watching from their porches. She's glad Mike is going out with Jennifer instead of his usual Friday night excursions with his drinking buddies. Maybe he'll stay sober tonight for a change. He'd better, or Theodore will have his hide.

Chapter 5

The drive to the theater is short, which is good as they are running late. Mike doesn't pay much attention to what's showing. His head is full of the day's events, and he wanders from his thoughts only long enough to admire the vision in his company this evening. Jennifer watches the movie intently and scolds Mike for disturbing her when he plays with her hair. The movie isn't over soon enough, and afterward the two make their way to the only pizza restaurant in town. Mike's diet here usually consists of pepperoni pizza and beer, but tonight, he passes on the beer. For most dates, the next stop is "make out point," nothing more than a wide spot on the side of the mountain road atop the city bypass. The view of the town below is pretty at night, at least until the windows are fogged over by heavy breathing. Tonight, though, Mike decides to take Jennifer to the only spot for recreation in town, the local bowling alley. Mike doesn't really care for bowling. Maybe because he was never any good at it and his pals made fun of the way he throws the ball down the lane, or because his mother spends so much time there on the women's leagues three nights a week. Jennifer doesn't care much for the sport either, but there really isn't much else to do in their one-horse town and the night is young. The two have some laughs at each other's expense on the lanes, and Mike forgets about the day's happenings. Two, then four games pass, and it's time to take his date home. The two laugh at their bowling prowess on the drive home, and reaching her porch, she asks him to join her on the wooden swing.

"I had a great time tonight, Mike," she says.

"Me too, Jen. Haven't done that in a while."

"Couldn't tell it by your performance. Really, I think you're ready for the pros," she ribs. Had one of his buddies said that, he'd be pissed. From her, it brings a smile.

"Boy, howdy. I'll be giving up this coal-mining gig any day now. Those pros better look out!" He runs with the thought.

"Nah, better not give up your day job just yet. Think you might want to break a hundred first," she continues. The day job comment quickly brings Mike's thoughts back to events at the mine, and he becomes noticeably quiet.

"What is it, Mike? Did I say something?"

"Nah, just thinkin' about today. Had to go see Mr. Stone. He asked me what I was going to do with my life. Go figure."

"Dad said he was going to talk to you. So what did you tell him?"

"Nothing. I mean, I didn't know what to say. He was going on about coal mining being a way of life and all. Wanted to know if it was in my blood. Wondered if I wanted to study mining at college. I told him I've never thought about it. Talked about being in management and all. That's a laugh. My dad would shit a gold brick if I ever became a boss. He's union to the core. I'd be disowned if I ever put on the white cap."

"Don't worry about what your dad would think. He'll deal with it. What do you think, Mike? What do you want?"

"I want . . . to go have a beer. The guys ought to be at the wall by now."

"Go ahead. Make a joke. Is working in the union and drinking beer with the guys all you want for your life? I thought you had plans."

"I did, Jen, but I fucked those up, all right?"

"So what then? You just going to quit? That doesn't sound like you, Mike."

"Ah, damnit, Jen. Give it a rest." Mike doesn't like the direction this conversation is going and feels his face becoming flushed and his pulse quickening.

"Then make some new plans, Mike. Things change, but life goes on. Roll with it," she adds in a pleasant voice. She sees Mike is becoming upset, and she doesn't want to end the evening on this note.

"When life deals you chicken shit, make chicken salad, huh?" Mike says, with a half-smile on his face. Damn if this girl ain't persistent. "Anyway, guess I ought to make some plans, set some goals toward something. Just ain't sure what yet. Hell, I ain't even sure this is what I wanna do with the rest of my life."

"The fate of the world doesn't have to be decided tonight. Anyway, it's nice that they think enough of you to speak to you about it," she adds as she begins to rock slowly in the swing.

I hadn't even looked at it that way, Mike thinks. "I did tell your dad I appreciate all he's done for me. He's a good man," he says as he looks Jennifer in the eyes. *Thank goodness she looks like her mom. But she does have her father's common sense.* "And thanks for goin' out with me this evening, Jen. I had a great time."

"Me too. Even if we didn't get to make out point," she offers slyly. The forwardness of her statement stuns Mike a little. But not too much.

"Maybe we can try and get there next time?" he asks through a grin.

"We'll see," she answers sheepishly as the front porch light suddenly comes on.

"I know what that means. Time to call it a night. Call you tomorrow?" Mike asks.

"Call me anytime, Mike. Talk to you soon." And she quickly gives him a peck on the cheek and disappears through the door.

Mike's happy with the way the evening went. While the tap on the face isn't what he was hoping for, he knew it was probably more than he should expect. This girl isn't like the other girls in this town. She is a class act—always has been. Tops in their class in high school, head cheerleader, heck, the girl even volunteered at the local soup kitchen on Sundays. Jennifer always had a bright and cheery disposition, was friends with everyone, and made it a point to talk to the underclassmen, which was something the seniors rarely did. It was as if she was separate from the other kids in school, almost on a whole other level. If that wasn't enough, all the boys were scared to death of her hard-assed father, which meant Jennifer never dated much in high school. College doesn't seem to have changed her much, either, Mike thought, and since she was going to be here for the summer, it'd be nice to spend some time with her. It was still early for a Friday night, so he revved the Mustang and headed to the local hangout to catch up with the guys.

Chapter 6

It was boom times for the West Virginia coal mining industry. McDowell County coal was a major source of fuel for steel production and electric power generation. The price of bituminous coal was going up, had risen almost 20 percent in the last year, and every coal mine was hiring. All of Mike's high school buddies who had not gone off to college, and there were a lot, had gotten jobs at the mines and were making good money. One out of every two people in the area worked in or around the mines. Coal mining has always been a boom-or-bust industry, and Mike was coming in during boom times.

Nowhere was the coal boom more evident than in Welch. The small hamlet, tucked into the narrow valleys created by the Elkhorn Creek and Tug River, was the county seat of McDowell County and the home of miners working not only at the Banner Fuels mine, but also US Steel operations in Gary and Keystone Fuels in Keystone. The town proudly proclaimed itself "the Heart of the Nation's Coal Bin." The miners were anticipating a huge increase in wages in the upcoming contract, and everyone was making, and spending, their money like these times would never end. The town was small, a little over three square miles in area, but had a robust population that had leveled off from the steady drop following the peak years of the 1950s.

Mike spends his evenings driving his Mustang all around the town. Down McDowell Street, Riverside Drive, Summers Street, around Lake Drive, all around Southwood, then back through downtown, up Tug Street where the toilet paper could be seen hanging from the trees lining the Tug River, marking the high water point of past floods, then turning up Stewart Street past the emergency hospital. If he felt especially daring, Mike would drive the one-lane road of Hobart Street around the mountain to Little Hobart Street and down the hillside past the National Guard Armory. Either way, the final destination was always the local drive-in. The drive-in was a popular gathering spot for folks Mike's age. The restaurant's bright flashing neon sign was the largest of its kind in the county. The place had the coldest Stroh's beer found anywhere. The only problem with Stroh's is its alcohol content. West Virginia is the only state in the nation where the beer has a 3.2 percent alcohol by volume. You have to drink a lot of it to get buzzed. Many miners stopped at the restaurant on their way home from the mine, still in their coal dust-covered work clothes, to get the first beers after finishing their shift. Coal mine gossip was as prevalent on the menu as the cheeseburgers and deli sandwiches. Coal miners have the peculiar habit of talking about everything but mining while in the mine, but talking about nothing else when outside of it. It's often said that miners mine more coal outside of the mine than they do in it and have more sex in the mine than they do out of it. Here, you could catch up on the happenings in other areas of your mine, how the other sections were running, and on more than one unfortunate occasion find out who got hurt, or killed, and what caused the accident. On the weekends, the stalls were often full, and you had to park up the street and walk back to the covered stalls and roam from car to car. Folks would gather up outside the vehicles, and late on Fridays and Saturdays, the drive-in was the site of more than one fistfight. Because of that, the police were often seen cruising around the property, but to their credit, they didn't interfere with the beer drinking or rowdiness, unless it got out of hand.

The drive-in closed at eleven during the week, one in the morning on the weekend, and you could count on the police circling after closing time until the crowd dispersed. Mike and his buddies would make the trip to the local convenience store, pick up a case of cold Stroh's, and head to "the wall." The wall was a long stacked stone wall outside a playground on Central Avenue. He and his friends have been congregating at this wall since they were in grade school, hanging out, playing cards and, as they aged, drinking beer and smoking cigarettes. The police drove by the place regularly, would slow to see what they were up to, but rarely broke up their assembly. If the police came by too often, the crew would take their beer and go to the old cinderblock shed inside the playground, out of sight from the road. The small building was nothing more than a brick dugout, open on one end entirely and roofed with tin. The inside had an old rickety wooden bench that sagged in the middle, and even though the structure was open, it smelled of mold and urine. You could count on someone being there on a weekend night, and most of the crew made their way there after dropping off their girlfriends for the evening. Alcohol was always present. In fact, it was almost sacrilegious to show up without some libation. Whether it was beer, Boone's Farm, Ripple, or something even stronger, everyone came with something to share. And the other unwritten rule was no one went home until the alcohol was gone. Many nights that meant they stayed until the sun was up.

The weekends were the only time Mike got to catch up with his buddies. That unfortunate aspect wasn't about to change with him going to the evening shift. Tonight he found three of his pals sitting in the playground shed.

"Police out heavy tonight?" he asked.

"They've driven by a few times," his friend answered. Mike knew by the twang in the voice it was Kenny Rogers. "Thought we'd come on inside and avoid any problem."

"Toss me a beer, Singer," Mike said to him. Singer was Kenny's nickname. Seeing how he had the same name as the country and western singer, it stuck. Kenny used to get mad as hell when they first hung the nickname on him, but he got OK with it once he started working in the coal mine. One of the quirky customs coal miners have is to give folks nicknames once they come to the mine. The lewder and more vulgar, the better. Mike knew of one man, a roof bolter, whose nickname was Catshit. His son came to work at the mine last year. The miners nicknamed him Kittenshit. Since Kenny already had one, the men didn't see the need to rechristen him. The man tossed him a Miller.

"What, no Stroh's?"

"Store was outta cold ones."

Mike pops the top and quickly drains the can.

Two other men were present in the shed. David Jacobs, also known as Runt, and Terry Williams, nicknamed Pecker. All three worked the midnight shift on the supply crew. The mine only ran coal on the day and evening shifts while the midnight shift had the responsibility of resupplying the sections with the materials needed to operate the next day. The supply crews were a laid-back bunch, and these three well fit that job description.

"So you gonna be with us come Sunday night, Mike?" Runt asked.

"Nope. The old man rolled me to evening shift. On Wildcat's section."

"Sonofabitch," Pecker added. "We's all planning on you being on our crew. But what the fuck? Evening shift? Damn, that'll kill your social life. Only shittin' thing you do on evening shift is work and sleep."

"Yeah, maybe so. But at least I'll get some sleep. It ain't natural to work all night and sleep during the day. I don't know if I could get used to it. I've seen you guys when you come out in the morning. You look like the walking dead."

"Who says you're up all night on owl shift?" Singer adds. "Heck, I think we all manage to get a little shut-eye some time or 'nother during the shift. Right, guys?" The other two grunt in agreement. "Ain't too many big bosses around during the night. We get our marching orders, deliver our supplies, then kick back. Easy gig."

"I want to get on a section and mine some coal. That's where it's at, man."

"To hell with that," Runt chimes in between swigs of beer. "Boss underfoot all the time, on your ass about the run throughout the shift. Something breaks down or the roof falls or the belt stops, then the boss goes hog-ass crazy. Then you gotta hustle your ass off to try and make up for lost time for the rest of the shift. Hey, I worked on east mains for three months. I know. Section work weren't for me. I was happier than a pig in slop when they rolled me to the supply crew."

"Well, I'm looking forward to it. Maybe get to learn to run some of the equipment," Mike replies.

"Run the equipment? Hah! Like that'll happen!" Runt chides. "The only fucking thing you're gonna do on the section is what you've been doing for the last six months. You'll shovel. Only difference is you'll have a helluva lot more to shovel at the feeder than you did on the beltline. The shuttle car operators hit that damn thing on the fly, dump their load, then head back to the miner as fast as the car will go. They don't give a shit where the coal goes, as long as their car is empty. They miss the feeder about as often as they hit it, and you'll be cleaning up the mess."

Runt doesn't paint a very pretty picture of section work, Mike thinks to himself. His report sounds nothing like what he's heard from his dad and uncles over the years.

"Anyway, at least you'll be away from that slave drive Theodore," Singer adds. "That motherfucker rode my ass for the entire six months I was on the day shift. I danced when my last day on his shift was done."

"But he has two fine-lookin' daughters," Pecker offers. "They gotta take after their mother, for that man is the ugliest motherfucker on earth."

That comment gets a laugh from everyone.

"How was your date with Jennifer?" Singer asks Mike.

"Fine."

"Get your finger wet?"

"She ain't like that, Kenny." Calling him by his given name was a sure sign to let this line of questioning go. Singer knew it too. So the conversation turned to cars, baseball, the love interests of the other young men, and what was planned for the rest of the weekend. The alcohol finally gone, the men made their way home.

Chapter 7

Mike can barely contain himself on the first day of his new assignment. It is different from what he had experienced his first day six months ago. Wearing his shiny new black hat, he climbs on the mantrip, essentially a large track-mounted bus, with the rest of the East Mains section crew. It's a tight fit for the twelve men, all wearing their mining gear and carrying lunch pails, but no one complains. The ride to the section takes a half hour, and many of the men catch a quick catnap.

Arriving on the section, Wildcat heads to the equipment while the rest of his crew make a beeline to the dinner hole, which is nothing more than a collection of buckets and empty cable spools in a crosscut at the end of the track. The men sit and break out a snack while the boss makes his rounds of the workings. It is a Monday, and everyone is unusually quiet, or at least it seems that way to Mike. In a few short minutes, Wildcat rounds the corner and comes to a squat in the center of the collected group, propping himself in a seated position on a short-handled pick hammer.

"OK, here's what we got," Wildcat begins, removing his hard hat and mopping the sweat from his enormous bald head. "The miner is in three, just got a cleanup to finish there. The bolter is in six and needs to be supplied. Two is ready, but one needs to be set up. Buggies are by the miner." Mike doesn't understand any of what the man just said, but heads nod in acknowledgment.

"But before y'all get started, let me take a minute to introduce you to our new feller. This here's Mike Thomas. Mike is Jim's boy. He's gonna be with us for a while. Y'all saw him briefly Friday. Mike, let me introduce you to the fellers you'll be working with. That big tall skinny feller over thar is Polecat Roberts, and sittin' beside him is Stinky Jarvis. That's the miner crew. Them two fellers leaning against the spool are Hamfat Hawkins and Bumpy Elkins, the pin crew. And over thar is Raceway Black and Leadfoot Hodges, the buggy men. That monster of a guy over there is BJ Meeks, and he is the bolter helper. And them two scrawny shitheads over there"—everyone laughs—"are scoop men Hound Adams and Skank Miller. My utility crew. Over there rummaging through his tool box is Sparky Todd." Each man nods as they're introduced, except Sparky, who, head down in his tool box, throws up one hand in a half-hearted wave. When Wildcat stands, the crew heads to their stations.

"Hang here with me, young'un," Wildcat says to Mike. "I know you ain't been on a section before, and I wanna show you how things are done before you get started." With that, Wildcat heads to the faces, Mike in tow.

Mining coal is not like it's shown in old movies. The picks and shovels, well, the picks anyway, are long gone. Coal mining is a highly mechanized process, and the workers who perform these tasks are highly skilled and highly paid. The mining process is a mechanized dance, where each step must take place in a specified order or the entire waltz screeches to a halt. Wildcat walks Mike through the process as they go across the section. The actual mining is done by the continuous miner, a machine that looks like a mechanical T. Rex. A continuous miner is an enormous machine, about fifty feet in length and weighing almost fifty tons, fit with a large rotating steel drum at its front, the drum fitted with hundreds of tungsten carbide bits that literally rips the coal from the seam. It is a loud, dirty, and violent process, ripping the ore from its seam. The loud gnash of the coal being mined, the clang of the chain conveyor, the hum of the machine's motors, and the whine of the shuttle cars create noise so loud it hurts Mike's ears.

Continuous mining operates in a "room and pillar" system, where the section is divided into a series of various-sized "rooms" or work areas cut into the coalbed, each work area called an entry and the actual area where the coal is extracted called a face. A continuous miner can mine over ten tons of coal a minute—more than a pick-and-shovel miner of bygone days could produce in an entire day. The entire process of the section revolves around the continuous miner. If the miner stops for whatever reason, things get shitty on the section, Wildcat says. If some other part of the process holds the miner up or, God forbid, stops production, things get worse. The mining machine dumps the extracted coal by a chain conveyor into large haulers called shuttle cars, electric-powered, rubber-tired vehicles that haul ten tons of coal from the face and then dump, also by chain conveyor in the shuttle car's bed, into a feeder. The feeder is a large metal holding container that slowly discharges the coal onto the conveyor belt Mike has become so familiar with. This device allows the shuttle cars to return to the face for another load while the feeder deposits the coal onto the belt, allowing for continuous production.

It takes a continuous miner about thirty minutes to advance into the coal seam twenty feet, or until the operator's cab is under the last row of roof supports. By law, the machine cannot advance beyond the roof supports. Plus, it is terribly unsafe. The exposed roof from the extracted coal is unsupported and very unstable and must be anchored before it is considered safe for traffic. Once the miner has reached this limit, it is removed or trammed to the next adjacent entry and the process begins anew. The roof bolting machine now moves into the newly mined area to install roof supports, or roof bolts. This roof bolting machine installs roof supports by drilling into the overhead rock, and the machine operator inserts either conventional metal rods or resin roof bolts into a predetermined pattern as approved by the federal safety inspectors. These bolts tie the roof strata together into one large continuous piece, much like nails are inserted into wood, to control roof falls. Roof bolting is considered the most dangerous job in the mine, Wildcat tells Mike. After the coal has been cut and the roof supported, the utility crew cleans up loose coal with a scoop machine, a funny-looking vehicle that looks like a dune buggy with a bulldozer blade. The scoop pushes the loose coal into the face to be loaded by the miner the next time it comes into this entry and applies rock dust to the coal wall to limit coal dust explosion hazards. It's the same rock dust Mike saw on the walls at the bottom of the mine shaft. It is literally applied everywhere. The support crew then hangs vinyl curtain to ventilate the working area, directing fresh air into the face to carry away coal dust and explosive methane gas. The entry now bolted, cleaned, ventilated, and rock dusted, it is once again ready to be mined. This process goes on in each entry, every day, advancing the mine twenty feet at a time.

"Your job on this section, young'un, is this," Wildcat explains, stopping to look the man squarely in the eye. "You'll help the utility crew when they need help, set up the faces, supply the bolter, help Sparky service the machinery, and when all that is done and there is nothing to do on the face, you'll work the feeder." With that, he hands Mike yet another Number 4 D handle square mouth shovel.

Holy shit, Mike thinks, *just like Runt said.*

He spends the remainder of the shift shoveling the spilt coal from the shuttle car conveyors back into the feeder hopper. After the first few shuttle car runs, it seems Raceway and Leadfoot are purposely missing the feeder. The two buggy men run their cars into the feeder, run the conveyors wide open until the bed is clean, and turning around in the car to face toward the miner, tear the hell out of there. The entire process takes just under a minute, leaving two three-foot-high piles of coal on either side of the feeder for Mike to clean up. He shovels frantically, but in just a few minutes, one of the shuttle cars returns with another full load, once again discharging its black contents into the hopper. For the rest of the shift, Mike fights an unwinnable battle against the cars, taking a break only long enough to choke down his lunch, then resuming his breakneck pace. The end of the shift doesn't come soon enough.

As the crew heads to the man bus, Stinky asks aloud, "Set one off today, boss?"

Wildcat answers, "I don't see why the hell not. New crew member is a special occasion."

With that, Hamfat, Bumpy, and Stinky go to the dinner hole and tap on the long green compressed air cylinders. "This 'un here's full!" Stinky says with obvious glee. The workmen unlatch the cylinder and carry it into the adjacent empty tunnel. Wildcat walks off back toward the faces, leaving the workmen to their fun.

Coal mines are essentially a series of long interconnecting tunnels, straight as an arrow. The engineers continually run sight lines to ensure the coal tunnels are cut as straight as possible. These tunnels run for miles and can take hours to walk. The track operates in one tunnel, the belt hauling the coal in another, and the rest of the tunnels are empty. Just long, dark, empty spaces. The workmen lay the compressed gas cylinder on the ground and place masonry blocks on each side of the cylinder, one each just below the valve and another toward the base. Stinky raises a sixteen-pound sledge hammer over his head while everyone else stands back.

"Fire in the hole!" he yells and swings the hammer down with all his might, breaking the valve protruding from the top of the cylinder clean off in the stroke.

Woosh! The cylinder takes off, careening down the tunnel like a rocket, blowing up dirt and dust in its wake. In just a few seconds, the cylinder is out of sight.

"Thatun's for you, rookie!" Stinky says, obviously pleased with himself. The men load up onto the mantrip and, with Wildcat's return, make their way to the shaft bottom. Most men sleep on the ride back, and Mike is no different. He is sleeping soundly when he feels an elbow to his ribs.

"Sorry about today," Leadfoot says. "We always make it hard on the new guy at the feeder the first day. See what they're made of. You done good. Lotsa fellers just give up, then we just ride 'em harder," he says through a toothless grin.

"Thanks," Mike offers.

"Tomorrow will be easier. We'll take it a little slower on the dump. Plus, Wildcat will start working you into the face more. Before too long, you won't have to spend much time at the feeder at all." Mike was glad to hear that.

"Speaking of the boss, where'd he go during the fireworks? That was something to see!"

"Boss had to make hisself scarce. Firin' off cylinder torpedoes is highly irregular and the company will fire you if'n you get caught. But it's somethin' we do on special occasions, like getting a new permanent crewman. So that'n was for you. Heck, Stinky would let one loose every week if'n Wildcat would let him. Last time we shot one off was when Hound got his divorce, almost a year ago now I reckon."

Leadfoot turns back over, the conversation done. Mike leans his head back against the mantrip wall. So now he's permanently on this crew. Well. He turns his hard hat down over his eyes and quickly dozes off.

Chapter 8

Mike has little problem adjusting to the three to eleven shift. He can stay up late after the shift is over, hang out at the local drive in until it closed then head back to his apartment, some evenings with whatever loose woman he might latch on to as the restaurants close. He isn't attached and isn't picky either. He is careful to not frequent the same establishments whenever he is out with Jennifer on the weekends. She likes his company, and he listens intently as she describes the events of her week, which consists of hanging out at the local pool, helping her mother around their home, and writing letters to her sorority sisters scattered around the northeast. He can sleep late without worrying about oversleeping and missing his cage. In the mines, you don't show up late for work. If you miss your cage, you miss the entire shift. Tardy isn't an option. Many a man has had to bid off the day or owl shift in fear of losing his job for missing too many cages.

One Friday evening as the crew is riding the mantrip back to the shaft bottom, Mike is trying to sleep but can't help but overhear a conversation between Hound Adams and Skank Miller.

"Snake handlers? You're shittin' me," Hound says in disbelief to Skank.

"I shit you not. Sho'nuff snake handlers. Copperheads, rattle-snakes. Big, fat ones. These fuckers go crazy and start passin' them damn things between 'em. They think the Lord will protect 'em."

"And this goes on around here?"

"Damn sure does. Little ol' church on the side of the road in Jolo, I hear."

"So you ain't never been there yourself?"

"Oh, hell no. Why would I wanna go there?"

"So you don't know it for a fact that this church exists?"

"Well . . . no. But I've been told."

"That's a crock of bullshit right there," Hound says. "No way there's such a place. Ain't no one in his right mind gonna handle poisonous snakes for fun."

"I say we go find out," Skank says.

"Fuck no! Why would I wanna go to a place like that, if it does exist? I ain't been in a church since my first hitch job, and since that didn't work out, I figured it didn't help none. And I damn sure don't wanna go to no place where they handle snakes . . . if there is such a place."

"You're just scared," Skank taunts back.

"OK, smartass, you're on," Hound answers. "But only if Mike goes." The crew still hasn't given Mike a nickname, which bothers him some, as a nickname means you've been accepted.

"So whatta ya say, Mikey? Ready to make a road trip to Jolo?"

Mike considers the offer silently. He too hasn't been in a church since high school. Most of the smaller churches in the area are Baptist. The larger churches are Methodist and Episcopalian while the largest of all is the Catholic Church, owing its largesse to the Polish and Italian immigrants who migrated to the area in the early 1900s to work in the coal fields. Mike isn't too fond of snakes either. In fact, he is petrified of them. Freezes up like a block of ice whenever one is around and has ever since he was a toddler in Kentucky. Seems his earliest childhood memories are of snakes: copperheads, rattlers, big black snakes, king snakes. His grandparents' Flatwoods, Kentucky, farm was covered with them. Mike had to fight the black snakes for strawberries in his grandpa's strawberry patch. A large black racer chased him up the path to his grandparents' farmhouse once when he was five. So, no, his initial inclination is to not even consider going. But the men have offered for the first time to include him in their adventure, and he doesn't want to look bad in their eyes. "All right," he replies. "When and where?"

That Saturday evening, against Jennifer's well-worded and -thought-out advice, Mike meets Hound and Skank at the

McDowell County Courthouse for the forty-minute drive up highway 52 to Iaeger. The two men look forward to riding in Mike's hot red Mustang, and Mike is glad to oblige. As Mike goes through the gears up Premier Mountain, he asks Hound the question that has been nagging him since the men began working together.

"Hound, what is that? You have a hound dog at home?"

"Nah. Hound is short for pussy hound. I'm just a hound dog, son!" the man answers, then sticks his head out the window and howls.

"What he means is he'll stick his dick in anything that moves. And he does. Hell, you can't throw a rock on the playground without hittin' one of his kids!" Skank adds.

"And I can guess where Skank came from."

"Shoot I reckon. I like screwing me some skank. Skanky women need love too!" Skank grins proudly.

In Iaeger, Mike turns the Mustang onto state route 80 to Bradshaw, then turns up Bradshaw Mountain on a very narrow and bending highway 83 to Jolo. West Virginia is the only state that legally permits serpent handling, and the most active serpent handling church in West Virginia is this one. The church sits about a mile up the mountain side, on the right side of the road. The church is a small white one-room building with not much more than a muddy wide spot off the highway for parking. The men exit the car, dodging mud puddles, and walk in through the front door. The church is modest on the inside as well, with paneled walls, ceiling fans, and signs forbidding gossiping, lying, and bad language from the pulpit. The church has five rows of pews on either side of the main aisle. In the back of the church is a wooden lectern, with a piano, two guitars, a tambourine, and a drum set off to the side and a line of small, wooden boxes on a platform in front of the pulpit. There are twenty people in the church, some men dressed casually, some in their Sunday best, the women all with ankle-length dresses and buttoned up to their necks, with long hair pulled behind their heads and hanging down their backs. Many come up and greet the three men warmly, yet the three do not venture off the back row of pews.

Some members of the church sit in front behind the pulpit. The service begins, led by an elderly gentleman with a long white beard.

The men begin playing the musical instruments. The singing and dancing is accompanied by a rhythmic, repeating, hypnotic drumbeat. This same song Mike tries to recognize is played over and over again, and the speed of the music and the level of excitement of the congregation increasing with each repetition. Suddenly, the wooden boxes are thrown open, and a man reaches down and brings forth a large, fat timber rattlesnake. Mike is quite certain it is the biggest snake he has ever seen in his life: six feet long if it's an inch, and big around as Mike's bicep. The music continues, growing ever louder and more fervid, and other believers take turns handling the snakes, some with more enthusiasm than others, their faces revealing a look somewhere between terror and awe. More snakes are removed from the boxes—copperheads, diamondback rattlers, cottonmouths—and passed among the congregation as they praise God and continue singing. The congregation moves rhythmically to the music, some speaking incoherently, dancing down the center aisle. The snakes are passed among the worshipers, but Mike can't hear them hiss or rattle. The elderly gentleman begins a sermon, himself ranting at a fever pitch, his face beet red, pausing only long enough to take a deep breath followed by a deep hacking sound that sound like a cross between a cough and an exhortation, each strange breath bringing the crowd to an arm-raising "Amen!" Mike watches some church members drink a solution of strychnine from a quart mason jar. He sees a woman member dancing up and down the aisle, holding a flame to her forearm.

Mike feels the sweat under his armpits and running down the crack of his ass. Whether it's the music, the actions of the congregation, the possessed fury of the jack-leg preacher, or the presence of the snakes only a few feet away, he turns and bursts out the church's double doors in a full run. Skank and Hound follow a few seconds later. Once they are outside, the two burst into laughter at Mike, sitting in his car.

"What the hell happened to you, fella?" Hound asks.

"Yeah, you looked like you were going to shit a gold brick in there," Skank adds, snickering.

"That shit's just too weird for me, man," Mike says in reply. He doesn't want the men to know of his deathly fear of snakes. Or that the entire scene reminded him a little too much of the funeral of his beloved grandmother a little over a year ago. She was a primitive Pentecostal holiness, and this type of worship was what she lived for. Without the snakes, of course. Three nights a week and all day Sunday, she went to these holy roller services. Her own funeral lasted for three hours. Mike tears out of the lot, spraying mud everywhere, burning rubber as his tires contact asphalt. He revs the car up through its four gears quickly, driving like a bat outta hell down the mountain. The two men convince Mike to stop in Iaeger for some beer, which the three guzzle on the drive back to Welch. Mike drops the two men off and heads for his apartment. Although it is still early for a Saturday night, he decides to call it a night, but takes the remaining beer home with him, which he polishes off quickly once in his apartment.

By Monday evening, the entire crew had heard of their Saturday night adventure. And Mike has his nickname. Snake. Snake Thomas.

Chapter 9

For Mike, the next few months run together into a continuous blur. His morning hours are spent hanging loose in his apartment. He's developing an addiction for television soap operas due to hearing the rest of his section's crew talk incessantly about their plot twists. The men discuss these shows as if they are talking about some family members. He heads for the mine at two, gets topside at midnight, and still has time for a last call beer at the Sterling Drive Inn. On really adventurous nights, he heads to the beer joint on Premier Mountain with Skank, but even though the place is open until three o'clock in the morning, he finds the establishment a little too raw for his tastes. The chicken wire in front of the bandstand is the first clue; the sand on the floor to dry up the piss, puke, and blood is the other. Cigarette smoke lingers in the air, the juke box plays a pitiful country song, empty beer bottles adorn the bar and every table in the joint, and the waitress serves longneck Stroh's with her country "can I hep U?" best. He'll hang around just long enough for a quick beer and to see if there is any loose strange, then he'll escape.

The female customers are all the same type. Old beyond their years. Rode hard and put up wet one time too many may be the most complimentary way of phrasing it. Rough-looking group. Virile females one and all.

A cigarette company came under fire a few years back for directing an ad campaign targeting what they termed "virile females." The type of woman who could kick any man's ass if she so desired. Hard drinkers, chain smokers, more prone to watch NASCAR than any soap opera. Can change a flat tire quicker than you can. Can drink you under the table. Wants to fuck you much worse than you want to fuck her. Likes tractor pulls more than football.

The two women Mike eyes this late night were the newer versions. Tattoos in the small of their backs. "Targets," some guys call them. "Tramp Stamps" are another, more endearing term without the vulgar connotations. Wearing blue jeans that are way too tight with their rolls lapping over the belt loops. Cigarettes out the side of their mouths, hanging as if it will fall out at any moment, but staying precariously put. You would not want to run into either of these women in a dark alley, even armed.

It was nearly closing time, and the old saying about how the girls get better looking at closing time was never more true. Mike also had a gut full of beer and there weren't more than a handful of women in the place, and the saying becomes more true. She was sitting at a table, all full of piss and vinegar with her girlfriend in tow, and after another couple of beers, Mike finally works up the courage to stagger across the floor to talk to her.

Two pitchers and a pack of cigarettes later, she's leaving the beer joint with him. To his luck, there was a flea bag motel not two miles up the mountain from the bar. It was closed but after incessantly banging on the door for fifteen minutes, the proprietor let him have a room. They had their way with each other, as best as two drunks could have in the shape they were in. It was one of those lustful one-night stands every young man dreams of but rarely truly ever experiences. Mike dropped her off at her car in the bar's parking lot at daybreak without any pretense of a call later. Hell, he doesn't even remember her name. A guy's perfect exit.

But pickup nights like those are few and far between. Most nights he is content to head for the apartment and crash.

Chapter 10

Mike works hard on the section. Wildcat has him with the utility crew, and Skank trains him to run the shuttle car, if only to give Skank some fuck off time during the run. The continual hard bump and jolt of the buggy across the rough mine floor is hard on Mike's kidneys. On the days he has to run the car for a full shift if Skank or Leadfoot is off, Mike usually pisses a little blood the next morning and his back hurts like hell. He's also spent some time with the bolter crew, but he discovers quickly that particular job isn't his cup of tea. There is a reason it's considered the most dangerous job in the mine. These guys have to secure the freshly exposed roof after the miner leaves. The temperature of the entry is hot from the continuous miner's motors and the friction metal against mineral during the extraction process; the roof creaks, pops, and moans as it settles; loose rock falls frequently; and the face hisses raw methane like a snake—Mike's new nickname. His job as a bolter helper is to set and move the temporary roof jacks, long and heavy metal tubes with large flat plates that are tightened between the floor and roof, also called the high wall and the foot wall, by ratcheting the plate against the roof using a hand jack, much as one would raise a car to repair a flat. It sounds good in theory, and the bolters have to set them by law, but in actuality, these flimsy metal bars aren't stopping the mountain if it decides to come down. The roof jacks are large, heavy, cumbersome, and severely impede the bolting process. Many times if the pin crew is behind, they simply ignore setting the jacks and just pin the top. On evening shift, where there aren't many big bosses or mine inspectors, a lot of safety laws get short shrift or outright ignored, and setting these jacks is one of those.

The high-pitched squeal of the metal drill bit under high-speed torque burrowing its way into the hard overhead rock makes most bolter operators wear large mufflers over their ears to protect their hearing. Same can be said of the miner crew. In fact, most of the communication on the coal face isn't done by voice, but by light. There is a whole language spoken by miner's cap light, and Mike learns it quickly. Come ahead (quick jerk of the head from left to right), back off (quick jerk of the cap light from floor to ceiling), stop (extremely fast movement of the head from left to right), all communicated with the movement of the miner's cap light.

Mike figures out very quickly where the action is on a working section: The miner. As Wildcat said to Mike his first day, the entire section operation revolves around the miner, and while Mike took the big man at his word that first day, over the past months he has come to appreciate just how true those words were. If the miner was running, if the coal was coming, Wildcat stayed away and let the men do their jobs. Let the machine have issues in a face, whether it be methane gas or problems advancing the curtain or problems with the top, then the boss became antsy. Let the buggies run a little slow, and he'd raise hell at the drivers. Let the miner break down, for reasons man-made or mechanical, and the otherwise-gentle giant would become a raving lunatic, ranting and screaming at the top of his lungs at anyone and everyone in earshot until the miner was once again operational. This was his programmed response at every miner breakdown, and Mike came to think his boss's response, and the response of his crew to him, was in a sense Pavlovian. Or else just excellent psychology on Wildcat's part, as it soon became obvious to Mike that the crew would do just about anything to keep the miner running. Miner low on oil? Fuck it, it'll get here sooner or later. Keep mining. Methane monitor cutting the miner off? Fuck it, cover the damn thing up with a sandwich bag. Keep mining. No curtain to advance? Fuck it, we don't need fresh air anyway. We'll just cover up the methane monitor. Keep mining. Rock fallen on the miner? Raise it to the roof and grind it to pebbles with the drumhead. The prep plant can separate out the rock. Just keep mining. And on more than one cut: hey, this is a good entry. The top is good, there's no gas, and the miner is running like a scalded dog. Why waste time moving this beast to the next entry? Let's keep mining. There were many nights where the miner crew only stopped mining when the buggy operators were under the last row of bolts and would then motion with their cap lights to stop and move on.

"I hate it when Polecat gets like this," Leadfoot said to Mike, who was hanging out with the utility crew on this particular evening. "The sonofabitch would keep on mining if we didn't say something. But be damn if I'm going beyond unbolted roof. I'll go along with most anything, but I draw the line there. Those two crazy motherfuckers are just plain lazy, that's all. Easier to just stay where they are than move the miner."

Which was true. Staying where they were made it easier on everyone else on the section, at least for a while. But when the miner moved after an extended illegal cut like that, it meant double work for the bolter and utility crew. Fifty feet to bolt and clean instead of the normal twenty. But over time, the crew came to understand and manage the spurts of effort in exchange for the extended break. In fact, these extended cuts became an unspoken expectancy. You had to start them early in the shift so the bolt and utility crew could cover the miner crew's tracks by the end of their shift. Heaven help the crew that didn't get the top bolted back at least to the normal twenty feet of virgin top. The shit storm never fell on the crew. They had a union for protection. No, the consequences always fell to the boss. Many a section foreman had lost his job pulling an extended cut, only to have the roof bolter break down, time run out, or in the worse-case scenario have the miner blow a cable or a track at the end of a fifty-foot cut, leaving the million-dollar machine exposed to a roof fall.

There is another unspoken rule in the mine: what happens on your section stays on your section. Crazy-ass stunts like extended cuts, cylinder torpedoes, and even small gas ignitions were kept quiet among the crew. Even the occasional fight between workmen was kept between the workmen. The combatants would disappear down one of the entries and work things out between themselves. Oh, sure, there would be whispers at the bar after hours, but most workmen were silent, and for good reason. On the section, it's just you and your crew. There's no one else. You looked out for each other. Your fellow worker looked out for you and you did the same for them. Getting outsiders involved would lead to no good coming from it. The upper-level management didn't give a shit. As long as the coal was coming was all that mattered. The union leaders didn't give a shit either, as long as they were getting their time in grievance meetings instead of working underground they were quite satisfied. And in the end, you'd still have to come back and face your crew. No, the only folks that mattered while you were underground were the men on your section with you. Mike came to understand this. Much like men in combat units, the only people you could count on were the men to your left and your right.

Mike takes the company up on their education offer. He returns to college that fall, enrolling at the local college thirty miles away in Bluefield while Jennifer returns to West Virginia University in Morgantown. Morgantown. It might as well be on the other side of the world as far as Mike was concerned. Morgantown was more a part of Pennsylvania than West Virginia. Seven miles from the Pennsylvania state line, only seventy-five miles from Pittsburgh. From Welch, Morgantown is over two hundred miles to the north, taking five hours by car along curvy, barely two-lane roads. Mike doesn't see himself making that trip. The one time he'd been there, as a senior in high school, was a frozen November weekend and he'd not enjoyed himself, so WVU never figured into his plans. Then or now.

Returning to college fills Mike's spare time. The two-hour round-trip drive, plus the two and three hours spent in class, forces the young man to become more disciplined, and he finds himself skipping the nightly beer runs during the weeknights, choosing instead to turn in after work. Eight in the morning comes very early when you work until midnight. He keeps his return to the classroom to himself, as he doesn't want to give his crew yet another item about which to rip him. No, this isn't about his crew or Jennifer or Mr. Stone or Mr. Theodore. He is going back to college to get the education his grandmother had dreamed of for him. He'd study all right, not what the mine bosses wanted but what he wanted. What that might finally be at the moment wasn't all that important. A college education is what he wanted. An education is something no one can ever take away. Perhaps one day he might, just might, want to get out of the mine and he needed another way to make a living. He needs an education for that. Besides, what the hell else was he going to do in this town? The rest of the folks could kiss his ass.

Chapter 11

While the Appalachian coal business itself was in boom times, the workforce was in turmoil. Tony Boyle was no longer running the United Mine Workers of America with his iron fist, and he was still a few years away from going to prison for the murder of union rival Jock Yablonski. The UMWA was now under the control of Arnold Miller, a rank-and-file miner who enjoyed tremendous popular support from the miners. While an honest and good-intentioned man, he was uneducated and in over his head as union leader of the hornet's nest of the UMWA. Into this power vacuum rose all sorts of vocal miners who thought they could lead the union but in reality would be no better than Mr. Miller if given the opportunity.

One of the basic tenets of all these competing voices was the desire—no, the "right to strike," as was the popular jargon. Basically what this demand meant was the local union officials could pull the miners legally out of work at any time they were unhappy with whatever issue struck their fancy. It was a damn fool demand, one any business owner would never consider. But this demand for a "right to strike" led to a whole lot of illegal "wildcat" strikes in the West Virginia coal fields in those times. Mike never understood it. "We're striking for the right to strike," was the cry. Hell, weren't we striking now? He didn't draw a full paycheck for months; they were always striking over something. The majority of the time he didn't even know why they were striking. No one else did either. Even the local union officers didn't. Someone would just say that there was a picket line at the road to the coal mine the night before, and that would wipe out work at the mine for the day. Mike's crew came up at the end of the evening shift one day to see no one waiting for the owl shift mantrip. The owl shift was on strike. Picketers at the road, someone said. But when Mike drove out the access road on the way home, the pickets were gone. If they were ever there in the first place.

Those "phantom picketers," as many liked to call them, could really wreak havoc on your paycheck. It was a long-standing tradition in the mines that "the shift that goes out is the shift that goes back." In other words, if the strike started on the midnight shift, as they almost always did by these phantom picketers, then the day and the evening shift would stay out in support of their union brothers until the midnight shift went back to work. So, basically, if something pissed off the workers on one shift, out they all went, until the miners that started the strike went back to work.

Mike was sitting at the mine portal one evening, getting ready to go down for the shift. It was five minutes until three, five minutes until the first trip of the shift. Suddenly, one young miner said aloud out of the blue, "Well, fellas, it doesn't look like we're gonna work today." He took the lid off his lunch pail and poured out his drinking water, which was sort of a sign that work was through. Every miner did that at the end of the shift when they hit topside. But today, he poured his water out before the shift started. And the shift was on strike, just like that. No one asked why. They just all turned around and went to the bathhouse, following the leader in a herd-like mentality.

Mike was certain many of these wildcat strikes occurred simply because someone was hung over and didn't want to work that day, so they kept everyone from working that day. He was young, without many bills, and could get by on the two or three days a week they were getting whenever they were working. So a free day off without any discipline for missing work was just fine by him.

One of the rumors going around the coal fields that summer was communists had infiltrated the union and were attempting to undermine the national economy by halting the production of coal. Now coal mines produce nearly as many rumors as they do coal, and this rumor had legs from the get-go. Mountain people are a close group by and large and, while quick to spread gossip, don't take to strangers or outsiders readily. That alone normally would be enough to squelch any such thoughts. But the influx of new people to the coal fields in the early seventies seeking big paydays made for a lot of strange folks in what had for years been small, close-knit coal camps. These new folks weren't from around here, so the rumors of communist infiltration were easily accepted. Miners, while they may be upset over working conditions or at the union leadership, are a patriotic bunch. They'd be no damn commies in our mines.

One summer weekend, a large rally was planned at a mountainside park just outside Premier and all UMWA miners (there really weren't any other kinds back in those days) were invited to attend to hear other miners discuss "the right to strike." A few of Mike's section workers and he bought a couple cases of Stroh's beer, loaded two coolers, piled in the back of an old pickup truck, and headed for the rally, scheduled for 3:00 p.m. The roadside park was packed to overflowing and three young, bearded miners were standing on a picnic table with bullhorns, leading the rally with exhortations of how evil and uncaring the coal companies were, how they were raping the land and sending the profits far away to other states while doing nothing to improve the plight of the folks in McDowell County. The folks in attendance, several hundred in all, were lapping it up, cheering at every word.

These guys were smooth, their voices commanding, their diction perfect. They said they were coal miners in Mingo County, and the plight of the workers there was no better. Yes, something had to be done to teach these profiteers a lesson. The companies were making record profits off the sweat and blood of the helpless miners. The workers were the power. We had to have the right to strike!

The crowd was worked into a frenzy, cheering every word of these three men. Then one of them said, "Now about this communist talk. Yes, there are communists in the coal fields. I'm proud to say I'm a communist, and the communist party has always been present to help the poor and oppressed."

The crowd fell silent, instantly dead quiet at this man's revelation. Then one lone voice from the crowd yelled, "You mean to tell us you're a communist?"

"Yes, I am!" the speaker replied defiantly through his bullhorn.

"Well, fuck you then!" was the response. And slowly the crowd began to disperse. Some remained, and the speakers resumed their oration, but the wind had been taken out of their sails.

A group of miners gathered about fifty yards away from the main group around an old 1950s Chevy pickup truck. That group grew larger as more and more people moved away from the speakers. Mike began to hear a rumble from this side group, and then they began to move in mass back toward the picnic table.

"Let's get these commie bastards!" cried someone from the crowd and the reformed mass charged the picnic table. The three men dropped their bullhorns and ran, but the mob caught one of them and threw a rope over a low-hanging limb above the picnic table. Holy shit! They were going to string this guy up! The noose was fastened, the man held upright on the table, and then the mob pulled the picnic table out from under his feet. Down he went.

Evidently the rope used to string the man up was as old as the pickup truck it came from. The rope snapped like a twig when the weight of the man pulled it taut. The commie speaker hit the ground with a thud. The crowd stood still, caught unaware for just a moment. That moment was just enough for the young man to jump up and run like a scalded dog down the hillside, arms and legs flailing madly as he escaped into the woods. To Mike's surprise, no one gave chase. The other two had already made their scalding exit, running wildly down highway 52, leaving their comrade to his fate. The excitement over, the crowd quietly dispersed.

Mike and his crew had not moved from their truck throughout the entire scene. There was beer to drink before it got hot.

"How about that shit?" asked Skank.

"Fuck 'em," said Polecat Roberts. "I'm only sorry that the sorry-ass rope broke."

Mike kept his mouth shut and kept on drinking.

Things slowly began to return to normal in the coal fields. The phantom picketers showed up less frequently, and the workers were getting full paychecks by the fall of that year. Some folks said that day in Premier the commies were taught a lesson and they had moved on to try and infiltrate other areas of the American economy. The truth was closer and more practical; school was starting back and folks needed money for back-to-school clothes and new shoes for their kids. The weather was turning cold and there was nothing to do and the heating bills would soon be going up. Mike returned to his studies that fall and forgot the entire affair. Except for this: Coal miners are a patriotic bunch.

Chapter 12

Coal mining is a self-defeating process. The company mines coal, which depletes their reserve, and coal is a non-renewable resource. So by extracting coal from its seam, the mine is in essence slowly putting itself out of business. When the seam is mined out, the mine is done. The company maximizes coal recovery and, thereby, their profits by extracting every possible ton of coal from the mine.

There are three methods of coal mining along a horizontal coal seam. The first is advance mining. Advance mining develops the entries for haulage, ventilation, and coal transport is the first stage and the mine is always in some way advancing itself out in all directions, moving farther and farther away from the portals with each cut. With each foot advanced, the cost for ventilating and maintaining the mine increases.

Once an area is developed, and to maximize coal recovery, the mine extracts the large coal pillars separating the entries in one of two ways. The newest method is by longwall mining, which hasn't made its way to the mine yet, but is rumored to be coming. The time-tested method of recovery at the Banner Fuels Number 10 mine is by pulling pillars. Pulling pillars is how the mine really maximizes coal production and profits, as the coal pillars are ripped from the seam using the same machinery that developed the entries in the first place. However, there is less cost involved in retreat mining, as it is called, as the roof is not supported and no further ventilation costs are accrued since both the roof supports and ventilation system are already in place. The area is not kept particularly well as once the area is mined out, it is abandoned and humans will never venture into that area ever again. They can't. The roof falls quickly once the coal pillars are no longer there to support the mountain above.

And that is the drawback. Once the pillars that were there to support the roof and keep the mountain off the workmen are gone, it is an absolute certainty the mountain is coming down. The best the miners can do is delay the inevitable long enough to retreat to a supported area and escape the falling rock. Coal mining is dangerous work in the best of circumstances, and pulling pillars ratchets up the risk. Only the most experienced miners work on retreat sections, but most of the workmen like working on these sections, as it is much sloppier mining than driving an advancing section. On a pillar section, there is no roof bolting, no rock dusting, no ventilation curtain to hang, no mountains of coal to shovel. Just mine coal.

Mike has spent the last few months working on Wildcat's section as a utility laborer, but on this particular night, their continuous miner is down and he gets assigned to work on a pillar section. The boss is a seasoned old foreman named Willie Bentley, who has been at the mine almost since it opened after World War Two. Which isn't unusual. Most of the retreat sections are manned by very senior men. Pulling pillars, while easier than advance mining, carries much greater risks, especially for roof falls, and the crews are usually seasoned coal mining veterans who work on retreat sections almost exclusively. Once an area is developed, the advance crew is moved to another area of the mine to begin development anew, while the work of extracting the coal pillars is left to the retreat crews. This is best, because these retreat crews are all older miners, set in their ways, and are not used to all the extra work needed on an advancing section. And they probably wouldn't do it anyway.

"So, come on, young'un," the old boss barks at Thomas. "Time to show you how to really mine some coal."

"Well, all right, then." Mike rises from his perch atop his round lunch pail and lets fly a mouthful of chewing tobacco juice onto the gravel. He grabs his pail and joins the crew on the elevator. Unlike Wildcat's crew who are always carrying on and cutting up on the ride to the section, this crew is quiet, and many of the men can be heard snoring in their seats.

Once on the section, the men go straight to the machines. No short break as the foreman examines the faces, for on a retreating section there are none. The men take a moment to look over their equipment, then the miner fires up.

"Thomas, you'll be working with the timber crew," Bentley says to him. "They're over at the scoop loading wood."

The timber crew on a retreating section serves the same purpose as a bolting crew on an advancing section. They are here to support the roof by sawing timbers, or trees minus their branches, cut the exact height of the entry and wedged tight against the mine roof. The timber's purpose is to slow the fall of the roof as the roof eventually gives way once the coal pillar is removed by the continuous miner. Slow, not stop. Nothing is stopping the entry from caving. Like the sun rising in the morning, once the coal is gone, you can count on the mountain coming down.

The timber crew works fast, using a hydraulic chainsaw to cut the tree trunks and quickly set them on either side of the entry, forming a wooden gauntlet to the coal pillar that the continuous miner bores into. While the miner eats away at this site, the timber crew sets timers and prepares the same gauntlet on the other side of the coal pillar. The crew will work one side of the coal pillar, then the other, taking a ten-foot wedge of coal from the pillar at a swipe until the entire pillar is removed.

Mike watches the process as he sets timbers. Pulling pillars is a much quicker process than mining on an advancing section. No bolting. No rock dusting. No curtain to hang. Cut coal, man. Finally, only two small stumps of coal remain, called the push-out. The timber crew sets two rows of timbers for the final push. Once the miner cuts the last of the stumps, the crew quickly backs the machine out of the area and into the safety of the entry between two solid coal pillars.

Old man Bentley eyes the roof line with the experienced eye of someone who has done this before a thousand times. Pulling a large piece of white chalk from his overalls, he draws a rough line along the mine roof.

"Set a double row here, boys, and make it damn quick!" he barks. The timber crew flies to work, the sawdust thick in the air and the tree trunks going up like they were sprung. In just a few minutes, there is a small forest standing between them and the mined out area. Mike is dripping sweat and soaking wet from manhandling the large timbers. The crew sets the last of the timbers when the large expanse of freshly exposed roof gives away, falling six feet solid and the concussion of the fall blows coal dust and sawdust thick into the air. When the air clears, Mike looks up at the mine roof. The roof rock broke along the exact line the old man had drawn on the ceiling. Only five feet away, the crew is safe under the coal block and behind the double timber row.

"That's it for today, boys," the wise old boss growls. "Let's load up and get outta here. Day shift can start the next pillar." The crew backs the miner up a little farther, set a few jacks around the miner for good measure, and leaves the section. *I could get used to this*, Mike thinks, but knows he'll never get that opportunity. Still, it was fun to just fly around and work in a different manner than he is used to.

Chapter 13

Three years pass.

Mike settles into a daily routine of driving the thirty miles to Bluefield for classes in the morning, then barreling to the mine with barely time to catch his cage for his shift underground. After working his ass off underground for a solid eight hours, he heads straight home after work, catching a few hours of shut-eye before starting the process over again the next day. And the next. And the next. He truly lives for the weekends, as that is the time he catches up on his studies, his laundry, his grocery shopping, and his sleep. One Saturday night, after a shortened shift because of a ventilation fan malfunction, Mike strolls into the lobby of his apartment building at 10:00 p.m. He's happy to get off work early as it is a Saturday and running coal on a weekend makes for an even longer week, so any off time is sorely appreciated. The elevator doors open and a tall, slender young lady with long, flowing blonde hair dressed to the nines exits carrying a bottle of expensive champagne. As the two pass, she gives the young athletically built man a long look over her shoulder, then turns to face him as he enters the elevator.

"Hey, fella. Wanna share this bottle with me?" she says with a low, sultry voice as she waves the bottle in her right hand. She sounds slightly inebriated.

Mike looks at her and gives her a grin. "Sweetie, on any other night I'd be all over it. But I'm whipped. I'm gonna call it a night, all right? Another time maybe?"

The disappointment registers on her face. "Well, OK. I'm in 3A. Come see me when you're rested." There is a hint of sarcasm in her voice. Clearly, this young lady isn't used to being turned down.

Especially by men. The elevator doors close, and shortly, Mike collapses in his bed, sleeping the sleep of the dead.

The mine ceases production for two weeks each summer. The annual miner's vacation is usually taken around the Fourth of July holiday, and Mike is especially looking forward to this vacation. He's heading to Myrtle Beach, the Hillbilly Riviera, for a week, meeting Jennifer there, who is traveling with some of her sorority sisters as a final farewell following college graduation. Mike has never been to the beach, has never seen the ocean, and is looking forward to taking a break from the mine and his grind if only for a little while. On the Friday before the two-week vacation starts, he is summoned into Mr. Theodore's office. He has never been in the old man's office, and anytime an hourly worker is called on the carpet usually isn't a good thing.

The old man's office is spartan. Just an old puke green swivel office chair and matching metal desk covered with years of ground coal dirt, oil, and sweat. A metal ashtray is the solitary article on the desk, overflowing with crushed unfiltered Camel cigarette butts. The only wall treatment is a large map of the underground workings, likewise covered with ink marks and smudge smears. There is a worn armchair adjacent to the desk, and Mike settles uncomfortably in it. The old man shuffles in, covered with coal dirt, and plops in his swivel chair. He lights an unfiltered Camel cigarette and takes a long drag, eyeing Mike. Mike is quiet, waiting for the weathered chief to say something, wondering why he's been summoned.

"So how you doing, Thomas?" the old boss asks, exhaling a large cloud of cigarette smoke into the air.

"I'm fine, sir," Mike answers nervously, trying to figure out what offense he's committed to earn a trip to the boss's office.

"Looking forward to the downtime? Got any plans for vacation?"

Mike doesn't know exactly how to answer. Does the old man know he's meeting his daughter? Is that why he's been called here?

"Getting out of town for a few days." It's all he's willing to offer.

"That's good. Man hasta have some time away."

Wildcat can be heard bellowing in the hall. "Snake! Where the hell are ya? Time to ride!"

"He's in here, Hatfield!" Theodore calls out. Wildcat peeks around the corner into the office and is surprised to see his laborer in the chair.

"What th' hell did you do, Snake?" the burly man asks, concern on his face.

"Nothing to trouble yourself with," Theodore answers. "Get a spare man from the belt crew. I'll send him up to your section later."

Puzzled, Wildcat nods and disappears. Oh, great, Mike thinks. He'll be the talk of the shift now. The coal mine runs as much on gossip as much as it does mining coal. Tongues will wag. He'll be fired in five minutes, disemboweled in ten to hear his section crew tell it. Mike suddenly gets a chill. Hell, maybe he will be fired. He still doesn't know why he's in the hot seat. As if the old man could read his mind, he speaks.

"How are your classes going?" he asks. Mike has never discussed his class work with anyone, especially the old man, but it doesn't surprise him that he knows. Mrs. Theodore and his mother visit almost daily.

"Fine, sir," Mike answers respectfully.

"Makin' progress, are you?"

"Slow but sure." Which was true. At the current, rate he'll graduate in another two years if he goes part-time year-round.

"Well, that's good, young man. Can't ever be educated enough." His comment surprises Mike. It was well known that Theodore never finished grade school, yet still rose to be the underground boss of one of the largest mines in the state. The mines had provided all the education he needed in his lifetime, and he'd learned his lessons well. Still, the old man was making small talk. *Get to it*, Mike thinks.

"Thomas, you've been with us for three years now. Three years underground makes you eligible to take the state mine foreman's exam. I want you to think about taking that test and becoming a supervisor here."

Mike sits, stunned. He had not thought about becoming a white cap. He was content for the moment with working on his section and going to school. He'd never even considered the possibility of crossing over and going company.

"You had to know we was goin' to talk with you about it. Thought that was why you were in school."

"Last I checked, the college didn't have any courses on bossing," Mike replies.

"Wouldn't think they did. That kinda knowledge you don't get in a textbook," the old man adds. *Now that's the old man I know*, Mike thinks.

"Well, I don't rightly know what to say, Mr. Theodore."

"Wouldn't expect you to right now. Just wanted to give you something to think about while you're away." *Does the old man know where I'm going or am I reading too much into this?* Mike ponders.

"You're too sharp to spend the rest of your days in the union, son. There's no future in the union. No way to get ahead. You're an hourly worker, and the only way you can make more money is to wait your turn and hopefully outbid someone for a better-paying job. No future in that, son."

"Well, OK," is all Mike offers. No need to say something stupid at this moment. With Mr. Theodore, he's always known it's best to say as little as necessary. "Reckon I need to get to work."

"Nah. Ain't nothin' happening on your section tonight. Wildcat and his crew will run coal for the first half of the shift, then spend the rest of the shift timbering the equipment. You won't be missed. Why don't you get a head start on your vacation? I'll see you get paid for the shift."

Mike perked up. He wasn't about to argue with that offer. It was standard procedure before a prolonged shutdown like the vacation period for the equipment operators to move their expensive pieces of equipment far away from the working face, park their machine safely in a crosscut between two coal pillars, and set timbers all around to protect the machinery from a roof fall while everyone was away for the two weeks. The thing about working on a section and mining coal is the crew is very good at that, but when you start asking them to do jobs outside what they normally do, things can slow to a stand-still. Wildcat would have to start timbering early if he hoped to finish by the end of the shift. Mike doesn't regret missing out on that chore. Plus, he'd heard of folks getting these "sweetheart" deals, paid time off on the down low, from time to time, but this was his first. And from the old man, the hardest ass in the company no less. Well, that'd be one for everyone to hear. Or maybe not. Don't need no reputation as some brown nose. Best to keep this one quiet.

"Well, thank you, sir. I'll take you up on it."

"No need to thank me, Thomas. Just seriously consider my offer. We can talk more about it when you get back from vacation. Now get the hell outta here."

Mike jumps up and bolts out the door.

Mr. Theodore calls Wildcat and tells him to not expect Snake, that he has the young lad working on a project. Wildcat knows better than to question him. Then Theodore calls his wife.

"Tell Jennifer I said she needs to talk to her feller when he gets there tomorrow. I suspect he'll have some things to tell her."

Chapter 14

Mike enjoys his week at the beach. Seeing the ocean for the first time is a lifetime memory for most, but for him, the experience borders on religious. The vastness of it, the never-ending surf crashing onto the shore, the timelessness of the ocean. It is impossible to feel anything but minute against it. The enormity of it initially places a small fear in Mike, but over the week, he comes to revere the ocean. Treasure it, even. He spends every free moment at the shore, sitting in a folded lawn chair with a beer in his hand and his bare feet in the surf, his mind free of any thoughts of the coal mine and Mr. Theodore. Over the course of the week, the ground-in coal dirt eventually washes from under his toenails. He relishes the smell of the sea, the slight twinge of salt water and fish in the air. I'd like to live near the ocean someday, he dreams. It is so unlike anything in the mountains. The open expanse, the nice hotels, the fancy restaurants, the multi-laned wide roads— nothing like this in the hills. When you pass north through the East River Mountain tunnel, it is as though you are stepping back in time thirty years to an altogether different world. Mike understands his world, but he'd rather live in this one.

He can't understand why Jennifer is returning home. Four years away, and now after getting her education degree, she's returning to "the free state of McDowell." She already has a job lined up as an elementary school teacher at the city's school not two miles from her home. Like the need for coal miners in the hills, there is an even greater need for professional people, and her dad's connections surely made the deal a slam dunk. Mike had been to Morgantown once, and it was nothing but a larger version of Welch, so he could see why in that regard her return was no earth-shattering decision. What he couldn't understand was her decision to come back at all. It's her home, she tells him, and that is what is important. He doesn't dwell on the question of her return, but after the first few days on the beach, after the new has worn off and they have exhausted themselves at The Bowery and on the Boardwalk, the conversation at a swanky restaurant one night turns to events at home.

"You've been picking at me about coming back home, Mike. How are things with you there?"

"Same old same old. Good to get away for a few days, though. I'm telling you, the grind can get tough at times."

"Still on the section?"

"Oh, yeah. Gettin' to do a lotta different stuff. Pay is good, and I like workin' for my boss and the guys."

"You've been there for a while now."

"Longer than I thought I would. But it keeps me in beer money and pays my bills, so I reckon I'll hang."

"So classes going OK too?"

"Hey, now, I really like going. The classes are interesting and the folks are a blast to be around. Don't see 'em but at school 'cause of work and all but they keep it lively there."

"Still studying business?"

"Yep, but I'm thinking about studying business education. Figure I can teach it. Become a teacher like you. Maybe coach."

Jennifer sighs. "Once a jock, always a jock."

"Darn straight. Life is a ball game, Coach Damron used to say. Figure I can be every bit as good at it as he was."

"You'd be better."

"Reckon that wouldn't take much. The guy was a womanizing drunk who didn't know his ass from a hole in the ground. All he did was yell at you. I don't think he taught me a damn thing."

"There is nothing you can't do if you set your mind to it, Michael," Jennifer says, looking him in the eye. "One of my dad's favorite sayings."

"Funny thing about your pa. He called me on the rug Friday before I left. Wants me to become a boss."

"Well, Dad seems to think a lot of you. Can't for the life of me understand why," she says good-naturedly. "He must. I don't think they extend that kinda offer to everyone."

Mike considers what she said. She was right. None of his buddies had been offered a bossing job, nor anyone on his crew.

"Maybe so. Still, don't know if that's what I ought to do."

"Why? What are you thinking, Mike Thomas?" Jennifer leans forward, placing her elbows on the table and her head in her hands, as if to say I've got time, tell me.

"Well, I gave it some thought on the drive down here. Not sure there is any advantage to it. I hear a boss don't make that much more than top union wage, but have to put up with a whole lot more shit."

"That is all my dad has ever been as far as I know."

"While my dad knows nothing but the union. Why, he'd shit a gold brick if I was to cross over."

"This isn't about my dad or your dad. This is about you. What do you want?"

"Hell, I ain't sure. I ain't sure I wanna be a supervisor. I ain't even sure I wanna be in that hole for the rest of my life."

"So you just gonna keep on doin' like you're doin'?"

"Don't see the harm in that."

"There isn't. But I thought you'd want more outta life, to make something out of yourself."

"Didn't say I didn't. Just not sure what that something is going to be. And what does that mean anyway? Make something out of yourself. Who judges if you've made something out of yourself? Is it you or those around you? Seems to me that judgment really ought to be the person's. Take old Coach Damron for instance. Folks in town thought his shit didn't stink, especially after we won the state championship. You woulda though he'd 'made it' wouldn't you? But the man had two outside children and could be found at the pool hall passed out drunk most evenings after the season was over."

"So how will you define 'making something out of yourself', Mike?"

"I ain't sure. But I don't think I'll take someone else's measure."

"Fair enough."

"And how about you? You've already made something out of yourself, girl. But how would you define it?"

"Probably not like most would either. Have a good husband that loves me for me. Raise good, solid kids. Have a happy family. I see my mom. She seems content. I think that would work for me."

Wow, Mike thinks. He'd always known Jen had a good head on her shoulders, but her views surprised him. And for the first time he actually thinks there may be a future for them— together. Still, he has to ask the question.

"If you feel that way, Jen, then why did you spend four years at WVU? If you wanted to get married, you coulda had any guy in our class. Then you could've spent the rest of your years cranking out crumb-crushers."

"Any guy in our class?" she says teasingly, giving him a playful look over her glass of wine. Then her expression quickly turns serious as she studies his question.

"Freedom," she says. "I went to school to be free. But not in the way most would think. I mean, my dad, I never heard him so much as raise his voice to my mother all my life, much less raise a hand to strike her. Yet I saw lots of my girlfriends in high school with drunken fathers that would verbally abuse their wives, and worse. I had one girlfriend who had to lock her bedroom door at night in fear of her stepfather beating her, and worse.

"My grandma had a saying she repeated to me over and over as a child. 'Girl, don't you get you no man 'till you don't need you no man.' I never understood what she meant until I saw some of those things happening to my friends, and their families. They were trapped, Mike. No job, no other place to go, left to make the best of their situation. Then I understood what Grandma meant. She meant I needed to be able to make it on my own before I tied myself to any man, so I wouldn't be trapped like my friends. It's why I worked so hard in school. Education is the key. I have a degree, and now a job. I don't need no man, as Grandma put it. I will make it on my own. So now I can get me a man—if I want."

Mike listens intently. There is so much more to this woman than he ever realized. She is right. Education is the key. For her, and for him. So she won't be trapped in a bad marriage. So he won't be trapped in the coal mines.

Chapter 15

The couple, if you can call them that, head back to the hills after the week at the beach. Like most folks on vacation, Mike feels rested and refreshed but still not ready to go back to work. There is another week of vacation to fill. He takes Jennifer to Grandview State Park one of the days, where they spend the hours hiking the trails and just staring from the overlook at the river below. That night, Mike sees his first live theater with a performance of *Honey in the Rock*, taking pride in the story of the state's founding. The two make three-hour drive back to McDowell County after the show instead of staying the night in one of the park's log cabins as Jennifer wanted. Dating the boss's daughter does carry some risks, and blatantly spending the night with her would be one sure way to piss him off. Not that they hadn't slept together at the beach, but they did have separate rooms there, and they were far away from the mountains. Getting a little close here, too close for Mike to risk it. Folks in these parts are old fashioned, and you just didn't pull that kind of stuff off in the hills without tongues wagging. He didn't give a shit about his reputation, but he wasn't about to put her through that gossip. And old man Theodore wouldn't take kindly to it either, of that Mike was absolutely certain.

The Sunday before returning to work, Mike goes to his parents' house for dinner. Sunday dinner had become something of a tradition since Mike moved out three years ago, and it was an opportunity for them to keep in touch with the goings-on in their lives. This was the only reason he went, as his mother was not much of a cook. Dinner usually consisted of pork chops, fried so hard you could drive nails with them, poorly mashed potatoes, and pinto beans. Every meal at the Thomas house had pinto beans as a side item. They were the one staple of his father's diet. Mike had eaten so many as a child he had lost any taste for beans and never touched them, except at his parents' dinners. Most dinner table conversations revolved around the happenings at the mine, and Mike thought tonight might be a good time to discuss Theodore's offer with his folks.

"Ready to get back at it tomorrow, son?" his father asked between bites. His mom's lack of culinary skills didn't bother his father. Either he'd grown accustomed to her cooking, chose to ignore how really bad it was, or his taste buds were burned out, Mike couldn't say which. But his dad shoveled down the meal without any hesitation.

"Don't reckon I've got a choice. Been good to be off these two weeks, though. What did y'all do while we were down?"

"Took your ma to visit her kin in Ohio. Damn shore is flat up there. Like the sky touched the ground. Me and your uncle even went to a Reds game. That was real fun."

"Sounds like it."

"Yep, but still couldn't wait to get back home. Your ma woulda stayed till the cows come home if I'd let her."

"She doesn't get to see her sisters as much since they moved to Ohio."

"Reckon that's so, and she coulda stayed, but there's no one there to bring her back, and it's a two-day bus ride from there to here."

"You could take some vacation," Mike offered. "You been there long enough. You got plenty of sick days."

"Nah, been sittin' 'round long enough. Time to get back at it. You still on Wildcat's crew?"

Mike thought this might be his opportunity. "Yeah, for now. Mr. Theodore wants me to go company. Become a boss."

Everyone at the table stops eating. It gets very quiet around the little table. His mother looks over at her son briefly, then looks quickly down at her plate. Mike's dad leans back in his chair and looks over at his son. "Now, why would you want to do something as stupid as that?" he asks, a touch of spite in his voice.

"Well, didn't say I do. But Mr. Theodore asked me to think about it while I was off, and I have, some," he answered.

"Why, that's the craziest damn thing I've ever heard," his father offers through a sneer, pushing back from the table. "Become a boss. No one in their right mind would do that."

"And why not?" Mike asks. He knew talking about this would get his father's dander up, but what the hell. No time like the present.

"'Cause any boss is just a damn lackey for the mine owners! I've been doing this for damn near forty years now, the last twenty-five in this mine, and I've had lots of bosses. Every one of 'em came outta the union. Traitors, I say. Don't none of 'em give a flying rats ass about their crew. They might say they do, but when push comes to shove, they'll do whatever their boss says do."

"Ain't it that way in any job, Dad? Everybody has a boss," Mike thinks aloud.

"I might have a boss on the section, but the union protects me. They look after my safety, see that I got a good wage and good insurance and all. You think the company would give me all that out of the goodness of their heart? Hell no."

"I really don't think they do all that, Dad. Safety is everyone's responsibility. You look after me. I look after you. I don't see the union helping me there."

"Son, you ain't been at this long enough. I remember when it was different, when the air was bad and the dust was thick and you loaded coal by hand and then to top it off at the end of the day the straw boss would try and cut your weight to pay you less. Wasn't until the union came through and organized us years ago that things underground got better. But that came at a price. The company brought in hired thugs to put down the union back in the day. Many a good man was hurt, and some were killed to unionize these mines. We fought hard and blood was spilled for these rights. You young bucks are just reapin' the benefits. Y'all don't appreciate where we was." Mike has heard this same line for years. It's his father's version of "when I was a lad, I had to walk five miles barefoot through the snow to get to school," except he didn't go to school so he couldn't tell that tale.

"All that may be true," Mike replies, "but I don't see how that applies to me today."

"Cause the company is still the company, son," his father answers, emotion rising in his voice. "They'll still screw you in a New York minute for an extra pound of coal. And you wanna be part of that?"

"Could be. I'm considering it." Not seriously, he thinks, until just now.

"I'm tellin' you, boy, it's a mistake. They'll use you up, and at the first sign of trouble, you'll be gone. They'll throw you off to the side like used shit paper. No security. None. In the union, I got me some security. I'm safe from being harassed by the bosses."

"Now, come on, Dad. Ain't no boss harassed you."

"Well, that's true, but they can't."

"See? You're a good man. Always there to work, never lay out and miss a shift. I've come to believe a good man doesn't need the union. He'll make it on his own merit."

"Don't need the union?" his father's voice raises even more. "Hell, every man needs the union. Even the bosses. If it weren't for the union, you think they'd have it as good as they have it?"

"You said a minute ago that the job was shit. Now they have it good. Which is it?" Mike's voice also goes up a notch.

"I mean with their pay and such. If we didn't make what we make, the bosses sure wouldn't make what they make. But they don't get the time off we get. They have to work whenever the company wants them to."

"I don't see you taking all that time off you supposedly get."

"I take my share of time."

"That's bullshit!" Mike almost screams. "You never take any time off. When I was in school, you never, ever came to a game. Not once in my years of high school did you ever come see me play. When I was a freshman, I'd ask Mom why you didn't come and all she'd say was you had to work. By the time I was a junior, I stopped asking. By the time I was a senior, I didn't give a shit whether you came or not. I took Mom at her word, that you had to work. I accepted it at face value, then when I started in the mine, I realized that with your seniority, you could've taken off pretty much any time you wanted. You just didn't want to. So don't give me a line about taking time off."

His father's face turns red. "I had to work. I had to pay the bills."

"Ain't nobody sayin' you didn't. It woulda been nice to have seen you there just once, just once. The only time you ever took off was for my graduation. I almost thought someone died."

"So now you gonna be a boss because I neglected you as a child? What kind of bullshit is that?"

"No, that's not it and you know it. I'm not real sure I want to do it. Just thought I'd get your opinion. I think I got it."

"No, you didn't, boy. But let me give it to you. Talk is, the company is bringing in a whole truckload of wet-behind-the-ears kids like you, young hotshots with just enough experience to take the mine foreman's exam. Ninety-day wonders, we call 'em. None of y'all will ever make it as a boss. You ain't got the experience. You don't have a clue about what you're doing. These crews will chew you up and spit you out."

Mike bristles. "So, Dad, in your opinion, just how much experience do I have to have to be a boss? Five years? Ten? How much time do I have to put in flunking around a section until I can lead a crew of men?" His dad's face is a bright beet red now. "You see, I don't think it's a matter of serving time. It's not like I have to wait for years in line for a better-paying job, then lose out on it at a bid only because someone has more time in the mine than I. In this system, in the union, it doesn't matter if I'm better at my job than the others, more capable. The only thing that counts is seniority. At least with the company, my efforts will count for something."

"Your efforts won't mean jack shit. The old man decides all, which is why every boss kisses his ass. Make this move and you'll see all too well. He'll have you by the short hairs."

"That may be so. But at least I won't spend the rest of my life tied to the same boring-ass job."

"That same boring-ass job, as you put it, fed and clothed you from the time you were a snotty-nosed baby suckin' on yo' mama's tit."

"And that was fine for you, Dad—"

"And your grandpa. Hell, he's probably turning over in his grave right now. I'm glad he ain't here to hear you talking like this."

"And Grandpa. Say you're right, that the union has been good to you, and it was to him. But it ain't enough for me. You may be right. I may well struggle at it. But I believe I want more out of my life than just laboring in the mine."

"Sounds like your mind is made up then."

"It wasn't, until just now. I'll show you. I'll be great at this."

"Just another ninety-day wonder."

"So you say." Mike pushes his chair back and tosses his napkin on the table. He looks over at his mother, whose head is still looking down, only now tears are dropping from her face onto her unfinished plate. He leans over and kisses her gently on the top of her head. "I'm sorry, Mother." He stands up straight, gives his dad a glancing nod, then leaves the house. His father sits quietly for several minutes, slowly shaking his head, then returns to his dinner.

Chapter 16

Wildcat sits atop a five-gallon oil can in the entryway across from the feeder at the belt. It is a strategic location, where he perches during the shift's run. Here, he can keep track of the comings and goings of the shuttle cars, and through their movements, he can deduce how the work is going on the face, without continuously traversing the section and irritating the men. Miners are a funny lot. If the boss hangs around too much, the men think something is wrong, or the boss is dogging them. So it is a fine line Wildcat walks, making sure the section is running smoothly yet giving the men enough room to do their jobs with relative ease.

"Miner done in three, boss man!" Leadfoot yells after dumping his load as he hightails his car back to the face. Wildcat checks his watch: seven thirty. Four cuts in less than four hours. The miner crew is rocking tonight. We might get eight cuts tonight if things keep going this well. Seven for sure. That'd definitely keep the old man off his ass for a shift or two. The miner crew seems to go much faster when Snake fills in on the mining machine. *I don't know what's got into that boy since we came back from vacation*, Wildcat thinks. It's like someone lit a fire under his ass. He's learned to run every piece of equipment on the section in the three years he's been here, and running some of the machines better than the men operating them regularly. Yes, sir, that lad has a real aptitude for coal mining, a real natural. It's in his blood. His dad is a real good hand, regular as clockwork, even if he does have a radical union attitude. Still, his old man isn't much different from a lot of the old hands. Thank God it doesn't appear the boy has taken up his father's views.

Wildcat puts a wad of Red Man chewing tobacco in his mouth and works it into a good juicy chew. What's really different about Snake is how he's taking to learning all there is to know about not only all the machinery, but about running a section. He asks about the ventilation, about the methane tests, about the time book. Damn if he didn't know better he'd think the kid was thinking about going company. Well, he'd have to have a talk with him if he might be thinking about that move. There's a lot more to running a section than just the mechanics of it. The nuts and bolts of mining coal is one thing. Handling a crew of cantankerous men, all with their own idiosyncrasies is something else. Still, the boy has the hustle, and one thing a boss has to do is hustle. Dealing with the old man would be something Snake has never faced in his life. The old man is the absolute best at tearing up fresh meat. You either sink or swim with him. There's no in between with the old man.

The buggy comes around the corner with the first load of the next cut. Five minutes to move the beast to a fresh cut. Man, that's moving. The men are really on a roll tonight. "Hey, boss, miner crew wants to know if we're running through lunch?" Raceway yells as he dumps his load in the hopper. Wildcat thinks only a moment. "Hell, yeah, tell 'em to keep it going." The old man would yell and scream about overtime when any crew is paid through lunch, but he'd only half-ass yell if there is a big run to back it up. And it looks like tonight could be that night.

"We're sumpin' it to the hilt, boss man!" Raceway laughs as he heads back to the face. The crew likes the overtime that comes with running through their normal thirty-minute lunch break, and a couple of lunch runs a week can make a real difference in a paycheck. Letting them continue can really build momentum for the rest of the shift, just as shutting down for a half hour really can kill a good run. After all, the half-hour shutdown is actually a good bit more than that. By the time the miner crew backs out, powers down, walks to the dinner hole, takes their thirty minutes, saunters back to the face, and then powers back up and restarts, it's actually closer to an hour. Sometimes the crew can make it up by hanging in a cut longer than they should, but it's a practice they shouldn't do, yet they're doing it more and more lately. That was one thing he really liked about Snake being on the miner. He didn't like taking those kinds of chances and would hustle to move the machine to a fresh cut instead of extending an existing cut. *It really doesn't make a damn bit of difference to me,* Wildcat thinks, *as long as we can get it bolted back up by the end of the shift.*

Wildcat thinks back to the foremen's pre-shift meeting today. Old man Theodore was in rare form, going on about production and overtime and the overall lack of effort on all shifts. How the hell he'd know about second shift was beyond him. The old man hadn't stepped underground on second shift in years. Truth be told, the old shit hadn't been underground that much on day shift either, to hear the day shift foremen tell it. Yep, the old man may be slipping. But he still runs the place with an iron fist. Cross him and you're gone. So the best way to handle the old man was to stay the hell out of his way. It has worked for the last five years and he'll just keep on doing things this way.

Wildcat checks his watch. Eight ten. Time to make the faces. He's supposed to make it across the faces every two hours, but hasn't been up there since making the faces at the start of the shift. The crew doesn't want him around that often, and especially if things are going well like they are tonight. No problem, I'll just backdate the plates like usual. Who the hell is gonna know? Now and once more across the section at the end of the shift, that'll get it done. He rises from his seat and goes first to the miner in the last entry. Snake and Stinky are extending the curtain, Leadfoot and his shuttle car waiting under the miner boom. Wildcat checks the gas level with his methane detector. All is good, well below the 1 percent level where they have to stop.

"All good up here, fellers?" he asks.

"Rockin' and rollin', boss man." Stinky grins. Wildcat writes his initials and time on the slate plate for this purpose hanging from a roof bolt, and moves onto the next entry. The bolter crew is on a roll, and only nods as he repeats the gas test in this entry. The utility crew is no different, barely acknowledging his presence as they prepare the entry for the next cut. The two entries on the left are set up and ready, and these two entries plus the one the utility crew is working on now oughta finish out the shift. Everything is rocking along. His rounds complete, Wildcat returns to his oil-can lounge. *I need to oil my rifle. Deer season opens this weekend, and I have a place all picked out on the backside of Premier Mountain. I've been putting down field corn for the last month, and the weather has turned cooler. Bucks like to rut in cooler weather. I'm sure to get one this season. I hope for a big eight-pointer like I got two seasons ago. Maybe take my son out there after the first week or so. He's getting big enough, and he's aching to try out the new .243 Winchester he got for Christmas. Maybe in a few years he'll progress to my .450 Marlin.* Wildcat smiles at the thought.

He wanders to the dinner hole. Sparky is stretched out on the cable spool, his hard hat down over his eyes, cap light out and snoring loudly. With the run the crew has going, the section mechanic has it easy. Really easy. There isn't supposed to be any sleeping underground, but like most laws and rules, the section boss is the ultimate enforcer on his section. Wildcat knows that if things should break down, Sparky will be up in a flash and busting his hump to get the equipment up and running, so he overlooks little transgressions like this. What happens on the section, stays on the section. Raiding his lunch pail, Wildcat pulls out a can of sardines and a pack of saltine crackers, eating them slowly, savoring the fishy, salty taste. He washes them down with a cup of steaming hot black coffee from his silver thermos and without disturbing Sparky returns to his oil can.

The shift is winding down, so Wildcat makes one more round across the faces. He is a little early, so he fudges the time on the slates ahead a half hour. He stops to talk to Snake.

"Finish up this cut, then move her to the next one if you have time. It's been a good run tonight. This'll be seven. Good job. Let's get the hell outta here."

It takes the crew a little longer than planned to move the miner, leaving them to run at a pace to the man bus. All hop on quickly, and Skank fires the engine. The tram picks up speed. Wildcat leans over to Snake.

"Good run tonight, young'un."

"Thanks, boss man. Everything just ran smoothly tonight."

"Seems to do that a lot when you're on the machine." Wildcat grins.

"Team effort," Snake says, nodding in appreciation.

"Now that's true. But the team runs better when you're leading. The miner crew sets the pace, son, and you do a set a good one."

"Well, I appreciate the bump. Now there's something I've been wanting to talk over with you . . ."

Chapter 17

Mike prepares all winter for the West Virginia mine foreman's exam. The weather really doesn't lend itself to many outdoor activities, and he has time now on Sundays to study. He hasn't spoken to his father since the dinner incident but does talk to his mother by phone every week. Although she gently prods him to come by the house, he makes excuses even he recognizes as lame. His efforts pay off as he aces the test, making the highest exam score in the state at that particular round of testing, and a first for the Banner Fuels Number 10 mine. He is rewarded by the company with a hundred-dollar bonus in his paycheck and is presented with a gold-plated flame safety lamp by Mr. Cone, the new mine superintendent replacing Mr. Stone, who was transferred a few months back to another of the company's mines in Pennsylvania. The company makes a big production of the presentation, and the picture of the two men shaking hands at the award ceremony even makes the local newspaper. Mike catches grief from his owl shift friends for it, and good-natured ribbing from his section mates, who seem proud this happened to one of their own. There is even a little celebration on the section to mark the event. Wildcat brings a white cake one evening, and the crew takes a longer-than-normal lunch to celebrate. This little gesture means more to Mike than the big to-do put on by the mine brass. At the end of the week, he is once again summoned to the old man's office for the talk he knew was coming.

"Nice job on the test, young man," Theodore says with a genuine sincerity Mike has not seen from the old man as he enters the small office. "That was the first time someone from our mine has scored highest on the exam. Tops out of a hundred men. Damn fine job. Needless to say, we're all proud of you. Especially Jennifer."

"Thanks," is all Mike offers. He always seems at a loss for words around the old man, and is especially uncomfortable when Theodore mentions his daughter. He figured the old man had to know they were seeing each other, but still he wasn't comfortable with her being brought into the conversation. She had been ecstatic when he told her the test results, and they had celebrated with a nice dinner at the swankiest restaurant in Bluefield. Mike decides to let the comment pass.

"Well, by passing the test, I reckon that means you'll be wanting a bossing job now?" Mr. Theodore continues as he motions for Mike to sit down.

"I still ain't sure, sir," Mike replies honestly, coming to a rest in the chair. "I like section work, running the equipment. I knew to become a boss I'd have to pass the test, sure, but as I got into preparing for it, I just wanted to see how well I could do. Wasn't anything beyond that."

"Well, you done good, no doubt of that," the old man says, lighting an unfiltered Camel. "Still, the company needs good young men like you. I need a construction foreman on day shift now. Patterson is going to retire, and the men on the other shifts don't want to come to day shift. Even though you don't have a lot of experience with rock and rail, I want you to take it. Do a good job there and I'll get you back on a coal crew as soon as an opening comes up."

"Well, I thank you, but I just don't know, sir."

"Know what? Don't tell me you're thinkin' of staying in the union!" The old man's voice builds. "Damn what a waste that'd be, son! Look, you're bright. You're steady. You work hard. Wildcat says you can run everything on the section, and that's no small task. Still there ain't no place in the union for your kind. The union is for a man who doesn't want any more out of life than an hourly wage. That's all. No future there. You might be years getting a bid for top wage. And then wildcat strikes can eat up whatever savings a man has put back. Any layoff comes and you'll be the first one to go, being low man in seniority and all. No stability in the union. No future in the union.

"More than all that, though, I had hoped you were made of different stuff. Am I wrong?"

The words cut Mike to his soul. "Ninety-day wonder," he says to himself. Or he thought he'd said them to himself. He must've murmured it under his breath, for the old boss hears the barelywhispered words and it brings out the fire in Theodore.

"Is that what you think? Bullshit, Thomas! Ninety-day wonder? I hate that damn term!" Theodore slams his hand down hard on the metal desk. "It's only used by the union men to deride a new boss, no matter how long he's been here, when truth be told, it's jealousy that one of them wasn't offered the job. A man that's willing to step up to the challenge and lead a crew of men, well, that takes something special. The job ain't for everyone. I readily admit that. Long hours some days. Lots of stuff to keep up with. And I know I can be a hard man to get along with most of the time. But I'll take a man that's willing to put himself on the line every day and accept the responsibility of production over the much larger number of men who lack the motivation or self-confidence or who are just too damn afraid to try. Didn't figure you to be one of the latter, Thomas."

Mike is stunned by Theodore's words. Now there is a different take on the situation than his father offered, and one that appeals to him. The old man leans over and looks the much younger man squarely in the eye.

"You ain't no ninety-day wonder, Thomas. You're the pick of the litter, son. Anyone that tells you otherwise is full of shit. They ain't seein' what I'm seein'."

That'd be my father, Mike thinks. At that moment, for the first time since the talk of becoming a foreman began months before, he had his answer.

"When do I start?"

Chapter 18

To conduct fresh air throughout the mine requires the construction of overcasts—brick and mortar buildings that allow polluted air containing methane and coal dust to pass over separated from the incoming clean air. Constructing these buildings means having large areas of overhead clearance, up to twelve feet in some cases. The normal way this headroom is obtained is by blasting the overhead rock, but blasting has its own problems. Blasting rock is different from blasting coal. By state law, only three pounds of explosive can be placed in a blast hole. While that is plenty to break up soft coal, when used in rock, it only serves to drop massive rocks onto the floor, which have to then be drilled by jackhammer and further blasted. A time-consuming operation. Another state requirement limits the number of blast holes shot at any one time to twenty. Again, plenty for shooting coal but an overcast typically requires upward of two hundred holes. Many times the drillers would drill the entire overcast for shot holes, taking several days, only to lose the majority of the holes from the roof shifting from the initial twenty shot blast, requiring the roof holes to be re-drilled. Another slow and time-consuming operation. The majority of these overcasts have to be constructed early on in a new section of the mine's development, so their construction often slows down production.

Whether the upper management saw the problem or it was just a quirk of fate Mike can't say, but there arrived at the mine a new construction foreman named Johnny Fountain. Johnny was a scrawny, rail thin old man from Logan County who was wrapped way too tight and cursed worse than any salty sailor ever dreamed. His sole job, as he likes to describe it, is "making little rocks out of big ones."

The man has absolutely no fear of explosives, in fact is absolutely in love with them and never misses an opportunity to make a boom. Instead of drilling large rocks before you blast them, as was required by law, he'd place a stick of dynamite under one, place a bag of rock dust over the unconfined shot, and blast away. This is called an open shot and is inherently dangerous. The construction crews loved him, as he made their jobs much easier, even if what he was doing was blatantly illegal. Mike really didn't care. Now that Johnny was here, he'd get to go run a section. The construction gig was different. The pace was slower than a section, and Mike missed the camaraderie of a production crew.

Now, the coal orders were steady so the mine no longer ran coal on weekends, and Mr. Cone decided to do all the blasting on the weekends when no one was in the mines. One weekend, Mike was assigned with Johnny to shoot twenty shots for an overcast. Now, this was no big deal to Mike, as he'd used explosives many times in the mines, both shooting coal and rock. He had become a certified shot-firer, as was required by state law if you handled explosives in the mines, at the same time as his mine foreman's exam. They were the only two men in the mine that Saturday, and loading and shooting twenty shots would take no more than a couple of hours, tops. With hustle, Mike thought, he'd be out in time to catch the WVU football game with Jennifer that afternoon. Mike didn't really care for WVU, nor Marshall where he'd gone for his first ill-fated semester. He was more of a Virginia Tech fan, it being only ninety or so miles down Highway 460. But as WVU was Jennifer's alma mater, he kept his allegiances to himself.

They went to the blast site. All two hundred holes were already drilled, and Mike knew the drillers would be there all next week, drilling it out again after he and Johnny screwed up their work with their shot. Johnny went to the powder magazine with a scoop to pick up the dynamite, but to Mike's surprise, he came back with two dozen boxes of dynamite and ten cases of blasting caps.

"What the hell are you doin', Johnny?" Mike asks.

"Figured we'd shoot the whole fuckin' thing. Hell, it's just us. Plus, I've always wanted to do one."

Now, Mike knew this was illegal as hell. There were two hundred shots there, ten times the legal limit. But by golly, Johnny was right. They were alone, and they could save their crews a whole lot of work if they brought the whole thing down at once. But what really got Mike to buy in was the "I've always wanted to do one" comment. What the hell, he thought.

Now, the legal limit for the amount of explosives per drill hole is three pounds. Each six-inch long stick of dynamite weighs a half pound. So six sticks filled three feet of hole. Each drill hole was ten feet deep. The usual procedure was to push the three feet of dynamite to the top of the hole, then use a clay dummy to plug the hole and hold the dynamite in place. Sometimes you'd place several dummies in the hole to make sure the dynamite was secure. It was best if the clay was wet, as it was easier to flatten against the side of the blast hole to hold the dynamite in place overhead. So, since they were shooting two hundred holes, Mike got a bucket of water and placed some clay dummies in the water.

The first stick of dynamite contained the blasting cap, then you placed the other sticks behind the initial stick and pushed the charge up into the hole with a wooden rod, and often two rods were needed as each rod was about five feet long and several of the holes were over ten feet in depth.

Now, while Johnny was quite reckless, he wasn't stupid. He knew how to handle powder and how to wire charges so the delays would build on each other and the net effect was to collapse the rock in rows from the center out. He started loading the holes with the dynamite while Mike's job was to place the blasting cap into the initial stick and hand him the powder. After Mike had given him the six sticks, he handed him a clay plug.

"Nah, hand me some more powder," Johnny said, tossing the plug back into the water bucket.

"How much more?" Mike asked.

"You just keep it comin', young'un." He grinned. He was having fun. He filled the hole completely, twenty sticks, then broke off a small plug of clay and plugged the end of the hole.

"That oughta make little rocks," he said, grinning wider still, and proceeded on to the next. Even though they worked fast, it took fourteen hours to load the shots. Mike had completely forgotten about the game, as he was at first excited about what they were doing, then became more nervous about the enormity of the shot and the possible consequences. They were putting their jobs and their licenses on the line, facing possible jail time, but Mike was young and brash enough to not care. Twenty shots at six sticks per shot was one hundred and twenty sticks of dynamite for a normal shot. When they were through, they'd loaded two hundred shots with twenty sticks of dynamite each, for a total of four thousand—four thousand!—sticks. Two thousand pounds; one ton of dynamite. They had to raid every powder storage magazine in the mine to gather enough. There was only one person on the surface, the hoist operator, and he was anxious to get home. He thought, as Mike did, that normally this was only going to be a couple of hours, but at the end of his eight-hour shift, he called in his replacement and must've called Mr. Theodore also, unbeknown to the two men underground. Two hours into the second shift, the hoist man called, wanting to know if there was a problem, to which Johnny replied everything was under control. What else could they say? They were way beyond turning back. Three quarters of the holes were loaded; it would take a day to unload the holes. They had to go. Finally, they were ready. Johnny wired the shot up and ran the shot cable out and around two pillars of coal.

Mike was shaking now. His mouth was cotton dry and couldn't make any spit. Johnny was absolutely ecstatic. He was about to make the biggest boom of his life. Mike was just hoping to live. Before Johnny wired the charge to the battery, he walked around the entire site one last time, checking the wiring, checking the surrounding area. He was crazy, but he wasn't careless or stupid. He called up to the hoist operator, "We're fixin' to shoot here. It's gonna be loud."

Then he came over to where Mike was, kneeling beside the shot battery. He ran the shot leads into the battery and raised the plunger. "You ready for this?" he asked, and in his voice Mike thought he heard just a little crack of doubt, as though he needed Mike to say it was all right to go ahead. All he could answer was a simple "Yep."

"Fire in the hole!" is the time-honored traditional cry of a shot fireman before he sets off the charge. It is a warning to let others in the area know what is about to happen. There were no other people in the mine, but it was just a habit all miners had. And before the shot fireman ignites the charge, he waits for the time-honored reply from anyone in the area that it is OK to shoot, and Mike gave it:

"Let 'er go!"

The plunger went down.

Their world went to hell.

Mike had never been in an earthquake, but he imagined this felt like being in an earthquake from inside the earth. Everything shook violently. Coal exploded from the wall of the coal pillar beside him. The concussion from both the blast and the massive amount of rock falling to the mine floor knocked both men off their feet. The air suddenly filled with a mixture of smoke, coal dust, rock dust, and debris stirred up from the blast. And they were five hundred yards away from the blast site and around two pillars. Mike just lay there on the mine floor. He didn't breathe. He just lay there trembling, like a cold, wet, scared puppy. He was quite certain they had just destroyed the mine and were on their way to jail for a very, very long time. He was finally brought back to his senses by the frantic screams of the hoist operator on the mine phone. "Hello! Hello! Y'all all right down there?"

Mike managed to walk to the shaft bottom and pick up the receiver, but he was trembling so hard he had to hold it with both hands. "Yeah, we're OK down here," he answered. That was all he could manage. Which may have been the truth. He sure as hell didn't know. The air was clear here at the shaft bottom, but up at the blast site, who knew?

Mike sat down, as his knees would no longer support his weight. His mouth was bone dry, but didn't have any water. He had begun to settle down a little until the mine cage hit bottom and off stepped Mr. Theodore. He was more than a little concerned.

"What the hell happened, Mike?" he asked. "That sounded like one hell of a blast." Mike couldn't answer.

"Just makin' little rocks outta big ones, boss," Johnny said as he rounded the pillar. He'd already been to the blast site. You could see the excitement and pride in his eyes. "Wanna see?"

The three men walked the five hundred yards to the blast site. What was normally a large, somewhat broken mass of solid stone the size of small cars, with dangerous large overhangs of rocks weighing a ton or more from an incomplete blast, was on this occasion a smooth pile of small rocks a hundred feet long with not a stone bigger than a teacup. And the top was as smooth as something cut with the miner. The smoke had cleared and it was evident that, while this was a nice job, it was huge, way too big for normal—or legal.

"Just what the hell did you two do here?" Mr. Theodore asked, now more than a little anger in his voice. Again, Johnny replied, "Just made some small stones, boss." That answer didn't seem to pacify him. "You two nimrods are gonna walk this entire place and see what kind of damage you have done to my mine."

The mine was huge, and walking the entire mine took several hours. It really surprised Mike how little damage there was. He was certain from the size of the blast they'd lost every brick-and-mortar structure in the place. There was one damaged stopping, concrete walls placed to direct ventilation, which he temporarily repaired with canvas. They both met back up at the blast site, where Mr. Theodore was still standing, this time with a quizzical look in his eye.

"You two assholes shot the whole damn thing, didn't you?"

They were busted.

"Yep." What else was there to say?

"Now why in the world would you two do something as foolhardy and reckless and downright dangerous as this without permission?" he asked. But Mr. Theodore knew as well as they the problems with working overhead rock in the mines. And after he was comforted by the knowledge that his mine had, indeed, survived the blast with no untoward ill effects, he settled down, and as time passed he looked almost content, like they had discovered something. Mike's stomach returned to its rightful location once the boss was placated and he too knew they hadn't destroyed the place. Mike was still sure they were going to be fired when they hit topside. To his surprise,

Mr. Theodore never said another word. Mike went home and slept for the next twenty hours. The stress had gotten the best of him. Johnny Fountain was promoted to head construction foreman the next week. The week after that Mike was sent to boss a section.

In the aftermath of their little adventure, the company filed a modified mine plan with the Mine Safety and Health Administration to shoot overcasts in their entirety on weekends when no one was in the mine, which was surprisingly approved. No one ever asked where the company got that brilliant idea.

Chapter 19

Mike squints his eyes as the elevator emerges from the hole. The sun always hurts his eyes at the end of the day shift. It wasn't something he had to deal with during his years on the evening shift. Everyone on the cage lets out a yell as the safety chains are dropped and the elevator door flies open. It was a habit, tradition almost, to acknowledge the safe end of another work day.

Mike walks slowly to the wash down hoses beside the rickety wooden benches. Most of the workmen exchange greetings with the oncoming shift, and Mike nods to a few of the men on his old section, then stops to give his counterpart on the evening shift the section report.

"Howdy, Tim. The miner's in number one. The bolter's in two. One of the shuttle cars is in the dinner hole with a flat, but the supply crew just dropped off the replacement at shift's end. The other car is running, though. The car of rock dust I ordered finally got there, but it looks like someone has pilfered some of it. The scoop has a hot battery on it, and there are plenty of oil, roof bolts, curtain, and other supplies. The miner shouldn't need bits for a while. Can't think of anything else. Have a good run."

"Nice job on that track entry crosscut turn."

"Thanks, Tim. Man, that was a booger. For some reason, the track entry was hot."

"Tell me about it. We were in a cut there night before last for an hour. Kept hitting gas pockets. Monitor kept shutting us down. I knew when it came time to turn it would be a bitch. Going against the curtain, instead of with it, was a gutsy move, but the right way to go. What did the old man say?"

"Nothing . . . yet. I haven't seen him. Don't think he knew before we went down this morning."

"Surely, he saw your mark up on the mine map."

"Maybe he overlooked it."

"Could be. The old man doesn't see as well as he once did. Anyway, nice move. Gotta go." Tim runs to the cage, getting on board just as the safety chains are being fastened. Mike reaches down, grabs one of the red rubber water hoses, and washes the black mud from his boots. Placing his round lunch pail on the ground outside the building, he walks into the foremen's office. The other foremen are working quietly, trying to hurriedly complete their reports and get off the property. Mike gathers his papers, time sheets, and fire boss book and settles into one of the metal folding chairs at the end of the small table he shares with the other five foremen on the day shift.

He is tired. The day's work was strenuous, both physically and mentally, and it shows in his coal dust-covered face. He too hurries and completes his reports, but the old man spots him before he can make his escape down the hallway.

"Hey, Thomas!" Theodore blasts. "Get your ass in here on the double. We've got a little business needs tending to!"

Mike once again enters the old man's office. Theodore was looking down at his section report from the previous day and, after a moment, began to speak in his low, gravelly, one-too-many-Camels voice.

"Thomas, why in the hell did you turn the track entry to the right? You know we turn all our entries in this mine in the same direction, to the left, into the line curtain. Why, the way you did it must've taken forty-five minutes."

"That's right, sir, it did. Actually more like an hour," Mike began. "But you know we've been having a lot of trouble with gas on our section. I thought it would be safer to turn the crosscut away from the curtain and maintain the air to the face. The other way is quicker, I know, but the methane monitor is always cutting the miner off. The gas just builds up way too quickly if the air isn't tight to the face. I don't feel comfortable when the gas gets that high."

"Well, then, damn it, put a sandwich bag over the sniffer head. Or just jump the damn thing out. There ain't that much gas up there. The monitor must be faulty. You can't mine any coal at that pace, son. You're paid to run coal now, that's all. Now, we've been doing things this way in my mine for all these years for a reason, and we'll keep doing 'em my way as long as I'm running this show. Don't let it happen again. Understand?"

"Yes, sir."

"Glad we have an understanding. Now get the hell outta here."

Mike burned under the collar as the old man carried on, but he dared not say anything, as he knew the old fart wasn't going to do anything anyway—at least not this time. He got up and walked quickly to the showers. The other foremen were already dressed and making their exits.

"So how was it, Mike?" Cal Ripley asked. "Didn't get too much of that ass, did he?"

"Nah. I'm still working here, so I don't reckon it was too bad," he says as he slings his hard hat across the bathhouse floor. The hat his father gave him is now painted white signifying he is a member of management, but you can barely see the white under the repeated layers of black coal dust.

"Don't let the old asshole get to ya. He's just trying to see what you're made of," Cal says, grinning. "Besides, it ain't like he's going to fire his future son-in-law." The remaining bosses burst out laughing at that comment. Mike has heard it before so many times since he signed over he's gotten used to it, so he just smiles good-naturedly.

"Anyway, tomorrow's another day," Cal continues. "We'll get it then. Catch ya later."

"Later on, Cal." Mike strips and jumps into the showers, letting the hot water wash away the grease, grit and grime, but more than that, washing away the events of the day. The shower is the best part of the shift, because it means it is over. He towels off and hangs his wet towel on the hook, then pulls the chain against the wall, raising his mine gear to the roof of the bathhouse. Here, the heat will dry out the sweaty, wet clothes overnight and helps keep down the bathhouse odors. His close-cropped head glistening with a mixture of water and sweat, he jumps into the Mustang, fires the engine, and scatters gravel around the parking lot.

He has his evening routine. He stops at the convenience store a mile from the mine portal and buys a six-pack of Stroh's, rapidly guzzling the first two without so much as a breath. Now with a small buzz working, he stops at the drive-in for a quick bite, which he eats as he drives to Bluefield for his night classes. He finishes off the rest of the beer on the drive. Most nights he has only one class, but the classroom takes his mind away from the mine, and Theodore, if only for a few hours. He rolls back into home around ten each night, just enough time to get his stuff together for the next morning. He then hits the hay, and if sleep takes its time coming, well, there is always a snort of Jack Daniels on the kitchen counter that helps speed the process.

Chapter 20

The drive to the mine in the wee daylight hours is the most peaceful part of the day. The fog rising from the valley settles into the tree-lined hillsides, awaiting the sun passing over the hilltop later to melt it away. The mountain air is fresh and clear, and Mike rides with the windows down every morning, no matter the temperature. As he rounds the last curve and sees the mountain of freshly mined coal at the preparation plant, he feels the first turn in his stomach. No doubt the Black Jack from last night has some hand in it. There will be plenty more stomach-churning moments throughout the day.

He had barely cleared the office doors when the old man spotted him. "I'm going to have a meeting with all you foremen as soon as you all are dressed and ready, so hurry the hell up and get out here," he barks.

What in the hell is it now? Mike wonders as he changes into his bank clothes. He mentally runs through the events of yesterday. Surely, he still can't be ill over yesterday. Mike is the first foreman seated in the foreman's office. He didn't want to do anything to set the old man off again. The other foremen wander in, and when the last of them have settled into their seats, Theodore limps in and begins to speak in his low, gravelly voice.

"Men, there are a few things we need to discuss and I need to get off my chest. So for the next few minutes, I want all of you to sit there with your ears open and your damn mouths shut until I get done saying what I want to say.

"We haven't run enough coal in the last two weeks to fuel a good fire. Now I read your reports every day. I see your markups on the mine maps. I see you all claim to have a lot of downtime, either from equipment or from gas, but I want each and every one of you to know, I ain't believing a word of y'all's bullshit. The reason we ain't running no coal is all of you have gotten sorry. You've come to accept these barriers and don't worry about them. Well, I do. When you get these things happening, then you have to work twice as hard to overcome them. I don't accept these excuses. Not one. You are put there on these sections to guarantee production. That is why you're all there. Maybe you don't care about your jobs anymore. I swear, I think we ran more coal back in the old days than we do with this high-tech machinery."

His face is a swollen red, veins bulging from his forehead and neck. He looks like his head might explode at any moment. "So, I want each of you to know, I ain't gonna put up with this bullshit. You can pick it up, or I will find someone who will. I'm going to be watching each of you a lot closer from here on, so either get with it or get gone!" He slams the door behind him, leaving the room, almost taking it off at the hinges.

The room is silent for a moment. "Well, the old bastard was sure fired up!" Cal Ripley nervously laughs. "I swear he's gonna give hissself a coronary if'n he does that too many times." All the foremen laugh a little, but inside they all know Theodore's word around this mine was law, and his ruthless reputation was well deserved. Stories abound that in his time as general mine foreman, he has fired a lot of really good men for one idiotic reason or another and wasn't bashful about doing it to any one of them. Mike's stomach churns some more.

It is getting close to mantrip time, and Mike makes a quick pass through the union bathhouse, checking to make sure all of his crew were on the job today. Today they all were. Getting fill in workers from the old man when someone was off was a real hassle, and with everyone here, it was just one less thing Mike had to worry about. Mike picks up his cap light, methane detector, and flame safety lamp at the attendant's station. He dials the burner wick up and, with a flick of his wrist, lights the lamp. Thick black smoke billows out the hood of the lamp, until the flame finally settles into an almost-unnoticeable blue glow. Picking up his lunch pail and water jug, he heads to the large, black steel cage.

Cal Ripley and Jeff Rose, two of the other foremen, are counting the workmen as they boarded the cage. The cage resembles a
large cattle car, and the two foremen made it look much more so by
packing the men so tightly on board until it seems the sides would
bulge. The workmen usually called for a headcount when Cal tried
to overload the cage, and today was no exception.

"Hey, boss man, you really trying to pack us on here this
morning!"

"Get off me, man. I ain't no fucking sardine!"

"Damn you're close. What's that sticking me in the back? Your
old lady should've taken care of that for you before you left home!"

"Headcount! Headcount!"

"Y'all shut the fuck up!" Cal finally orders over the drone of the
workers. "I don't hear any of you fuckers calling for a headcount in
the evening when we're trying to get up from below. Now fasten the
chains and let's flush this toilet."

The safety chains were secured and the cage begins its descent,
slowly at first, then picking up speed until just short of a free fall. The
trip to the bottom seems short, much shorter than the ride out in the
evening. The cage slows abruptly, then crawls for the last forty feet to
the landing. As he steps off the cage, Mike looks up the circular shaft.
The twenty-foot diameter opening at the surface looks no larger than
a penny from this depth. Just how far was it to the surface? It really
doesn't matter, he reckons. Whether five feet or five miles, there's still
rock over your head, and it will kill you if it falls on you.

Mike and his ten-man crew make their way to one of the man
buses at the shaft bottom. After arguing over which bus was theirs, a
daily occurrence, the crew loaded up and began their twenty-minute
ride to their section. Mike always rides in the driver's compartment
with Lou Reed, his miner operator. He does it to keep Lou from
driving like a bat out of hell back to the cage at shift's end, but as they
were going to the section, Mike knew he didn't have to worry about
Lou's driving habits.

While the crew gathered in their dinner hole, a makeshift set
of benches situated around a trash can and a single overhead fluorescent light, Mike goes ahead and scouts his section. The section crews

always stopped at the beginning of the shift to eat a little something before the hard workday ahead. The old man would have a hernia if he knew the crews were doing this, but it has been a practice in the mine for as long as anyone could remember, and Mike was sure it would royally piss his crew off if he ever tried to get them to the face sooner. But the old man's rant made him at least consider it. Mike walks quickly across the section. Miner in three. Bolter in four. Shuttle cars ready, one behind the miner and one at the feeder. Good. The midnight shift is supposed to set the section up to run for the day shift, but the push for production of late has led the midnight crew to also cut coal, and Mike was the one who usually had to suffer for it. Maybe today would be better.

He walks quickly back to the dinner hole. The section was set up to run, and the old man would know it soon enough. Before much time would pass, Theodore would be on the mine phone yelling for him, wanting to know if he was loading coal. In the dinner hole, Mike stops to look at each of his crew, pauses for a moment, then begins his daily speech.

"Miner crew, Lou and Kate, miner's in three. Full cut. Two and one are ready. Take it from there.

"Pinner crew, Jeff and Dave, bolter's in four. Five is down too. Y'all handle it.

"Buggy boys, Mitch and Larry, one's behind the miner, the other on the feeder. Hope they're running.

"Service crew, Reggie and Gary, scoop's on charge. Right side to service as soon as the pinner gets done in four. Pinner needs some bolts, though, first thing.

"Randy, check the spare scoop battery for charge. The owl shift ran up here last night, so I hope we're in good shape. All right, that's it. Let's have a good run"

"You're getting better at your morning speeches, boss," Kate Matthews, the miner helper, says slyly as she passes him. She was the newest to the crew, one of the few females working in the mine, and the only female miner helper on any shift. There had been somewhat of a stink when she won the miner helper bid, and the union even went so far as to ask for a second look at the bids, to make sure no one more senior had submitted a bid for the job. Mike didn't know what to make of her yet, whether she was just kidding with him or making fun of him. But she was a good worker who did her job and didn't complain or cause trouble, so she was OK by him.

Mike had only been with this crew a few weeks, and he was slowly beginning to figure out the little idiosyncrasies of his crew. Except for Kate.

Chapter 21

Months pass.

Mike's schedule changes little. After work, four days a week he goes evening classes. Bluefield State College is a small commuter school, located on the side of a hill above the large Norfolk and Western railway yard in Bluefield. Most of the students are working during both days and evenings, so to accommodate their students, the school offers almost the same set of classes in the evenings as are offered during the day.

Due to the nature of his job and the time it requires, he misses a lot of class lectures. Fortunately, most of the material is in the required readings, and he gets notes from several sympathetic classmates. There are lots of courses where he only shows up for the midterm and final exam. Class attendance in college fortunately isn't mandatory.

The final of his business economics class is on Monday evening at seven o'clock. As usual, he wolfs down his dinner in the car on his way to Bluefield, but that habit along with the Stroh's beer and the Mexican food on this particular day has produced a tremendous case of stomach gas. Cramping gas. "Bend over" gas. "Need to go sit on a commode and let the gas off" gas. But it's a final exam, an essay type test where he has to write pretty much continually for two hours. There's no time to take a break and go to the little boy's room. So Mike thinks, *Heck, I'll just let off a little SBD here.* You know, silent but deadly. So holding his bowels as best he can, he slowly and quietly lets off a gas attack. It is silent, but goodness is it deadly. Mike can barely stand the odor, but he keeps his head down and continues writing furiously. He decides to check the classmate behind him to see if he noticed the stench. Mike turns his head ever so slightly to get a partial view of his classmate whose head is likewise down and he is writing madly, but his face is a beet blood red. Yep, he noticed.

Finishing his test before his classmate behind him, Mike hands in his paper and gives the professor a note, asking if he would give it to his classmate when he hands in his test. The professor says he will. Keeping his word, the professor hands the student the note after he has turned in the assignment. He opens it and it says only: "Sorry. Once we get the chance, dinner is on me. I owe you."

Sometime after one of their next classes, both he and Mike have a good long laugh. And dinner. Just not Mexican.

Chapter 22

Theodore sits behind his desk listening on the mine phone as the section foremen call the preparation plant the start time of their section's coal run. He keeps a mental list of the sections that have called in. Cal Ripley calls in first. Cal is a good man. He has been at the mine over twenty years now, and Theodore has watched him grow from a green trainee to his best section foreman. He knew he could count on Cal to do whatever he said and whatever was necessary. Jeff Rose calls in second. A good man, a hard worker, but he wonders if Rose has the mental toughness to be bossing a crew of men.

Mike Thomas was now calling. Seven thirty-five, about the right time for him, but his section was in really good shape this morning, or so the owl shift foreman had said. He wonders if it was such a good idea to bring Thomas to the day shift. After all, the day shift was meant to be a promotion for a job well done or for lengthy service to the company. Thomas had not been in the mines all that long, and he had pushed him to take the salary job, after all. Hell, even getting the boy a job at the mine was a favor to his father. Ordinarily, Theodore wouldn't consider doing a favor like that for a union man, but they were neighbors after all, and he'd watched Mike grow from a snotty-nosed kid playing kick the can on the streets outside their home into the strapping young man he was now. He had always been an athletic kid, and Theodore used to watch him play on Friday nights, then critique his performance on Sunday mornings before church service. Placing him on day shift in the construction foreman job had filled a need and gotten his daughter off his ass. Evidently she wasn't getting to see her boyfriend enough, but his move to the day shift didn't seem to improve that little problem either. He knew

Thomas was driving to Bluefield every evening for college classes, and while it seems to put a crimp on his daughter's social plans, so far his studies had not interfered with his job, which was good. Going to school was all right, but nothing is to interfere with the job. If push ever came to shove, the school would have to go.

Perhaps putting him on a coal crew this early was a mistake. He was doing a good job on the rock crew, and getting to know the entire mine, not simply a single section of it. That knowledge would come in handy if he ever became a shift foreman or more. And supervising the supply crews, the belt crews, and the track crews is not as demanding as the constant, daily stress of production. *No, he has to learn it the way I did, the hard way. If he's going to be a boss for me he'll have to be tough. I'll go pay him a visit today*, Theodore decides, *show him my way of doing things. The kid would appreciate it.*

Roy Estes calling in now. He checks his watch. Seven fifty-five. That's almost an hour since going underground. Even with his twenty-minute mantrip ride, that's forty minutes late. That's a cut of coal. *I can't live with that*, he moans. He reaches over and pushes the pager button on the mine phone.

"Roy! What in the hell is the matter down there that you can't get cuttin' before eight o'clock?" He holds the pager button down so that everyone throughout the mine can hear what he's saying on loudspeaker.

"Miner was low on oil, Mr. Theodore," the boss explains. "We had to get more oil from the end of the track before we could get started."

"That's bullshit, son," Theodore bellows, still holding down the pager button. "I could've pissed the oil tank full and still been in the coal by seven-thirty. Why the hell didn't the owl shift oil the miner? It's their job! Get with it, Roy. You've got time to make it up." He hangs the phone up quickly, not waiting for a reply. None was needed. He'd made his point. *That man really hacks me off. Bullshit. Plain ol' bullshit. It's all I ever get from him. That fellow has been the second biggest disappointment to me in the time I've been running this mine.* Which made him think of Harry.

Harry Jones had been hired in on the day shift over a year ago. Theodore had planned on sending him to owl shift, but Jones was tight with the super. Members of the Moose lodge or Mason's or some such bullshit organization Theodore had never had time for. Now, Mr. Cone rarely ever questioned, let alone interfered with Theodore's decisions when it came to the underground workings of the mine, which was why Theodore didn't squabble when Mr. Cone asked Theodore to place Jones on the day shift. It had wounded the pride of some of the older foremen, a new boss stepping into the preferred shift, but that's the way it is when you're on salary. Seniority goes out the window. Hell, they all knew that. Still, even his being on day turn could've been accepted if Jones had been a real gunner, a top producer, or a real dyed-in-the-wool company man. But the fact was Harry Jones was probably the worst foreman that Theodore had seen in quite a while. The man never, ever got onto his men. They all loved him, for Christ's sake. He paid them through lunch every day, but his production wasn't any better for it. Gave his men special treatment too. He'd often bring a cake or a cooked ham for the crew, or hand out those stickers for the hard hats the machinery service reps would give to the foremen. Who does he think these people are? They work for him, not the other way around. Going easy on them all the time only leads to no good. Before long they'll be running the section, and that just wasn't gonna get it. Now here it is over an hour after going underground and Jones hasn't started running yet. *Just like I said this morning, they're down there fucking off. Something's got to be done. I can't allow this slack performance to go on. It may rub off on some of the other crews. I'm going down there right now and nip this problem in the bud. Helping Mike Thomas will have to wait.*

He rises slowly from his seat, straps his mining belt below his rounded belly, picks up his walking stick, and heads for the cage. Snuffing out his stogie and loading his jaw with a plug of chewing tobacco, he lowers the cage gate and sends himself into the pit.

Henry Jones calls the preparation plant. His man bus had jumped the track on the way to the section, but his crew was loading now.

Chapter 23

One of Mike's favorite excursions is to the barber. At this point he still has some hair on top, but like most coal miners who wear a hard hat for the majority of their waking hours, it was thinning. His favorite barber on McDowell Street gave his customers the hot towel treatment, neck massage, close razor shave, everything an old-school guy could want from the grooming experience. It was a two-chair shop with the old spinning barber pole out front, a real throwback to an earlier time, not like the newer unisex shops in Bluefield.

This particular Saturday, Mike had a barber he'd never seen before, which was outside his comfort zone. A little concerned, the service started out as he expected, but then this new barber commented, "You know, your hair is thinning."

"Yeah, I've noticed," Mike said.

"You've got a few strands that reach across your head," the barber said, continuing to snip away with his scissors. "It's perfect for a toupee. The clips would catch these strands perfectly."

Mike had never even thought about a rug. Every one he'd ever seen looked like shit, so unnatural, so this was not an option.

"Nah, I don't think so," he replied.

The barber kept cutting, talking about how a toupee would give him a different look, restore his youth, yada yada. Restore his youth? *Hell, I'm only 26!* Mike told him he wasn't interested a couple more times while he finished his trim and applied a hot towel to Mike's face.

When Mike thought they were finished, he just sat there, relaxing, enjoying the heat from the towel. As he rose from the chair ready to go, the barber said, "Wait just a minute. I want you to look at something for me." He disappeared into a back room and shortly reappeared with a rug in his hands. It looked like a dead rat.

"I think this will look great on you," he says, approaching Mike as he stands in front of the barber chair.

With a sudden rage, Mike leaps at the man, grabbing him around the neck and pinning him against the wall. His face inches from the barber's he said, his voice coming between clenched teeth, "If you come near me with that piece of shit, I'm gonna shove it up your ass. Do we understand each other?"

"Yes, sir," the barber answers, a deer-in-headlights scared look on his face. Mike calmly releases his neck. "That's great . . . How much do I owe you?" he asked, pulling the drape from his neck.

"No charge, sir," the barber says, trembling.

"Thank ya," Mike replies. And then he calmly walks out of the place. Man, is he mad. How many times does someone have to say no? He told the man to let it go. *I think he got the message.*

Chapter 24

"That's all, buggy!" Kate yells to Mitch as the continuous miner smacks into the finished mine face. Mitch jumps out of his seat and quickly turns to face toward the feeder. In just a second, he's racing down the narrow entry on the way to his dump on the feeder. Lou backs the miner out of the face and piles out of the cramped cockpit. He and Kate jerk up the yellow plastic canvas and hammer it into the last roof plate. Done in this entry, it's time to move on. The crew has this move from entry to entry down to a practiced science. Kate watches the huge electrical cable coil and uncoil as Lou trams the machine as fast as it will move to the next entry. Mitch and Larry string out behind Kate, hoisting the power cable to the roof using strong metal wires looped through specially designed holes in the roof plates. By the time Lou has the miner in the next face, Larry already has his shuttle car under the boom of the beast, ready to be loaded. The way this dance unfolds is a sight of wonder to Mike. He ran a miner in his time, so he is well aware of the effort needed to move a miner quickly and appreciates his crew's finesse.

"Here we go, buggy!" Kate yells as Lou starts the huge motors necessary to turn the steel drum on the front of the miner. The relative quiet of the tram from one place to the next is quickly replaced by the loud whine of the motors and the clanging of metal against metal and metal against rock. As Lou jams the tram lever forward, the miner crashes into the solid coal face, producing a terrible grinding noise and causes the fifty-ton machine to bounce up and down as it eats its way into the ore, bucking not unlike a wild bronco ride. The friction of the metal coal bits against the roof causes sparks to fly, lighting up the coal face better than the fluorescent lights on the side of the machine ever could. The miner's metal conveyor spits the crushed coal out with such a speed it resembles a black waterfall as the coal falls from the conveyor boom into the hopper of the shuttle car. In just a minute the twelve-ton shuttle car is full, and Larry wheels his pickup truck on steroids out of the entry.

Mike sits at the mouth of the entry, the last intersection twenty-five yards behind the mining machine. It is less cramped here than in the face where the machine is working, and from here he can keep an eye on the run without being in his crew's way. He looks at his watch as Larry pulls his car into the tunnel. Two o'clock in the afternoon. In their ninth cut at two. This will do it for the day. A record run. After the twenty-minute cut is complete, the miner crew backs the machine out to the intersection and powers down. Lou checks the drum for bad bits, and he and Kate swap out a few broken bits while Mike calls the preparation plant with the day's total.

News travels quickly in a coal mine, like shit through a goose. By the time the crew reaches the shaft bottom, the entire shift knew about their record run.

"Gunner! Gunner!" the other foremen chime as Mike and his crew boards the cage. A nine-cut run was the most anyone on the shift could remember. It was definitely the most he'd ever been a part of, either working on a section or as a foreman. While the workmen talk back and forth as the cage makes its trip to daylight, Mike looks over at his miner crew, Lou and Kate. The two were standing side by side, but unlike the others carrying on, these two stood in silence. Several folks pat them on the back, offer words of congratulations and the like, and Lou would smile and give a short reply, but drop it just like that. Mike knew he was not much of a talker, and Kate, well, he still hadn't figured her out.

Mike walks over to Lou as he is washing the mud from his boots. "Lou," Mike says, stopping him in his tracks, "I just want to say thanks. Y'all done real good today, and I appreciate it."

A huge toothless grin comes over Lou's face as he replies, "Just put it on my paycheck, boss man. See ya in the morning." And he disappears through the double metal doors into the union bathhouse. Mike's step is very lively into the foreman's office.

"There's the gunner!" Cal whoops. "Nice run today, young'un!" He pats Mike on the back a couple of times and sits down beside him and they begin to fill out their paperwork. Within a minute, Theodore comes stomping into the foreman's office. The stench of his stogie fills the room and the heavy smoke encircles his head as he speaks.

"Well, today was a little better, men. I see my talk the other day must've done some good. But we still got to get better. Still too much downtime. You've got to get your people to work harder. There just isn't enough production. We've got orders to fill.

"Mike Thomas, you got mine patrol this weekend." The old man leaves the office, but the stench of his stogie remains.

Mike sits there, stunned. The rest of the foremen just hang their heads and smirk.

"Reckon dating the old man's daughter does have its benefits, huh, Mike?" Jeff Rose tosses the barb at Mike, but he's too dumbfounded to pay it any attention. Well, if that doesn't beat all, Mike thinks. Here we've had the best run ever seen at this mine and the only thing the old bastard has to say is work Saturday. No good job, well done, no comment about the run at all. Just work Saturday. The elation Mike had felt at the run was gone. The old man sure knows how to fuck up your day.

He hurriedly finishes his paperwork and quickly showers. He just wants to get as far away from the place as fast as he can. The Mustang slings gravel high into the air as Mike tears out of the lot toward the convenience store. Two quick beers make him feel better, but the dejection doesn't leave him this evening, eating at him on the drive to Bluefield, in his class, and it is his last thought as he lays his head down for the night. What a hard ass. How can he be so stone cold and his daughter be so much the opposite? Then a cold shiver goes down his back. What if she really isn't? What's the old saying? The apple never falls far from the tree? He sleeps an uneasy sleep that night as the thought continually runs through his head.

Chapter 25

Mike's crew continually advances the section, twenty feet at a time. Running two shifts every day advances each entry about 460 feet a week. Mining coal is a hard process, ripping mineral from rock.

One shift as Lou is advancing the mining machine into a cut of coal, suddenly the face seems to explode. But it isn't a gas explosion; it's coal that seems to literally explode out toward the miner crew.

"What the hell?" Lou exclaims as he rapidly backs the mining machine up. The explosion of coal is rapidly followed by a deluge of water, covering the drumhead of the machine. Seeing this, and not knowing what to make of it, Lou and Kate work frantically to back the machine even farther away out into the nearest cross entry, then around a corner. The water continues to flow rapidly, covering the floor of the entry very quickly in three inches of water.

"Go get the boss and make it quick!" Kate calls to the buggy operator, who quickly turns in his chair and tears out.

He doesn't have to. Mike has heard the muffled sound of what he thinks was an explosion and catches up just as the minor clears the corner. Lou and Kate are soaked through with water and wet coal.

"Are you two all right?" Mike asks nervously. The two are drenched to the bone, not in sweat but with cold water. A loud din, sounding a lot like water passing through a pipe or air passing through a tunnel is emitting from the face, a hundred feet up the entry.

"Y'all stay here. Let me go check this out, "Mike says as he shines his cap light cautiously up the entry. Wading through the now six inches of water on the floor. The turbulence grows louder as he approaches the face.

Ten feet from the face, standing under the last row of roof bolts, Mike sees the issue. It's something he's never seen before: a plume of water about a foot in diameter is rushing from a hole in the roof where it joins the coal face. Lou cut into this, releasing the water from above.

Mike checks the methane level with his handheld device. Well within normal. He advances the line curtain to the last roof bolt to make sure the fresh air reaches the face, then wades back out of the entry to his crew. They are all standing around the mining machine.

"What the hell is up, boss man? "Dave asks.

"Damnedest thing I ever saw, "Mike replies, bewildered. "Lou must've cut into a water pocket or something. I've never seen anything like it. Y'all mosey on up there and take a look if you want to. Just don't go out from under the bolts."

While the crew goes to check out the unexplained phenomenon, Mike calls Theodore and explains the situation. Not knowing exactly what to make of what he's been told, Theodore arrives on the section half hour later. He gets an indication of how much water is flooding the section by the small river that is now running down the track as he approaches.

Water in the coal mine is nothing new. All mines have to deal with water. Whether it's ground water breaking through from the overhead rock or bubbling up from the floor, to leaks in the water main supplying water to the sections, to the water being produced by the continuous miner, all mines have water problems. so all mines have pumps. And all mines have union employees called pumpers to handle the water. The pumpers are quickly called to the section. Many of them have been on the pumping job for decades, and to a man, they've never seen anything like this.

Water behaves underground just as it does on the surface: it seeks the lowest level. Mine engineers will run elevations to generate underground topographic maps so management can see where the low-lying areas are. These will become water reservoirs or sumps as they're called underground. Often times the nearest sump is an abandoned area of the mine and the water is just pumped into that area. In this case it's not hard to figure out where the water reservoir is.

You just follow the water until it starts accumulating. Which for this section is about a mile down the track. A large underground pump is installed, and the water is pumped to the nearest sump. The section crew is pulled from the section to start laying the mile of collapsible pipe.

Theodore and Mike walk to the entry where the water plume is located. The sound emitting from the hole due to the constant rush of water is almost deafening.

"OK, Mr. Theodore, you've been around and seen it all. What the hell is this?" Mike asks.

Theodore works his chew and strokes his chin in thought. Letting fly a stream of chewing tobacco, he answers, "It's a core drill hole that wasn't plugged." Mike can only shake his head. The son of a bitch truly has seen it all.

Theodore turns matter-of-factly and goes to his Jeep and leaves the section, leaving Mike to supervise the pumping chores.

When Mike gets to the surface, Theodore is waiting for him outside of his office. "Hustle up and get changed. There's something you and I have to see." Rapidly completing his paperwork and showering, Mike returns to the mine foreman's office. The two men jump into a company jeep and drive north.

"Once I got outside, I called Mr. Cone and told him what was up. He put the mine engineers on the problem. Seems they located the unplugged core drill hole. That's where we are going now."

They drive for several miles over rough terrain, down a logging road requiring the use the Jeep's four-wheel drive. Finally, they come to a clearing that looks to have been strip mined, with a small creek running through the area. Exiting the jeep, Mike can hear a loud sucking sound, like water going down a drain. Walking to the creek side, he sees a whirlpool of water going down a hole in the ground. He knows where that water is going.

"It's a comedy of errors really," Theodore says. "The company drills core sample holes in advance of where we're going to be mining. These samples tell us how thick the seam is, what the roof might be like there. Just gives us a general idea of where we're going to be mining. Once the core drill sample is gathered, the hole is supposed to be backfilled with concrete. So that when you cut into one underground, you never notice., and even if it wasn't backfilled, that's usually not a big issue. The holes usually collapse on themselves and fill anyway."

"They drill core holes in water? "Mike asks, puzzled.

"No, of course not. This creek wasn't always here. So they could strip mine the area, the company diverted to creek from over to our left to where it is now and unfortunately right over the unplugged core drill hole."

"Son of a bitch," is all Mike can offer.

"Yep, it's a real cluster fuck," the old man replies. "Of course, the company is making efforts to fix it now. The bulldozers will be here tomorrow to redirect the creek again. Then the core hole will be plugged. You ought to be back running on your section in a week."

"In the mean time?" Mike asks.

"I'll find something for everyone to do. Probably break up your crew for a few days. Looks like you'll get to do some mine patrol."

Mike nods. Great. Just great. Scut work.

Chapter 26

The last few weeks have been hard on Mike, moving his crew from section to section in an attempt to mine coal, and most days splitting up his crew to do fill in work on other sections while on the surface, the construction crew tries to repair the core drill hole so Mike can get back to his regular roost.

Coal miners are no different than the rest. We all have our normal routines, which are so ingrained that when these are disrupted our psyche seems to suffer. Mike's attitude is further damaged as Theodore makes him his temporary personal flunky, having him run errands and overseeing things in the mine that the old man either doesn't have time for nor the inclination to do.

Never one to make his college classes regularly in the best of times, in his current mental funk, he neglects to go for several weeks altogether. Which is a shame, as without the section paperwork to complete, he has plenty of time to make his classes. Then, he suddenly remembers he has a business economics final that night.

Arriving harried just a few minutes before the test, he sits at his desk as the professor passes out the exam. Reading over the first page, Mike doesn't have an answer for any of the questions. Flipping through the pages, he sees this is the case for the entire twenty-page exam. He drops the test back onto his desk and stares at the pages. Dejected and totally demoralized, he tries to think what he should do in this moment. Feeling sorry for himself won't do, nor is it his way. He decides he'll just tell the truth and let the chips fall. If he has to repeat the course, well, graduation will just be one semester further off. Which is a shame because he is getting so close. So close.

Calmly strolling to the teacher's desk in front, Mike puts his paper down, looks the man squarely and firmly in the eye, and tells him, "Sir, I am not prepared to take this test tonight." Not knowing what to expect, the words that come from the professor are a shock.

"What can I do to help, Mr. Thomas?"

Dr. Randolph Harcourt Richards is a kindly old professor and looks just like you'd draw one if you could. Full, scraggly beard and bushy eyebrows that look as though they could overlap his silver metal glasses, behind which hide eyes possessing a spark that belies his years.

"Well, sir, things have been a little hectic at work of late, and I haven't studied as I should've."

"I see," the professor ponders. "Young man, here's the deal. I have to turn the grades in on Tuesday. Could you be ready to take the test on Monday evening?"

Mike jumps on the gift immediately. "Yes, sir, I can. And I promise you I'll be ready."

Professor Richards smiles. "How about promising me you'll try to make a few more classes in the second course in this series next semester?"

Mike hangs his head. Busted. While attendance may not be mandatory, it seems the professor does keep it in his head.

"Yes, sir, I can do that." And he means it. It is the least he can do to repay the man who is clearly going out of his way to help him. "Thank you, sir."

"Nah, no need for that," Professor Richards says, waving his hand away. "I know you and most of the folks in these night classes are working full-time. Heck, I did it too, all those years ago. I was a fire boss in the old Pocahontas mines, where the coal was twelve-foot high if it was an inch. Figure you oughta get a break sometime. But, Thomas, this is a one-time deal. Next occurrence, you're shit outta luck."

"Understand. There won't be a next time," he promises the professor and himself.

"You're a section boss, right?" the professor asks.

"Yes, I am," Mike answers. "How did you know?"

"Your look," Richards replies. "You look like someone who is burning the candle at both ends and in the middle. Most of the union workers in these classes look tired, sure, but not as spent as you look. You been bossing long?"

"About two years now, I reckon," Mike replies. He could figure out exactly how long, but he just whips a number off the top of his head.

"So plan on continuing to boss after you get your sheepskin?"

"I don't know. Why?"

"Because it's been my observation that mine bosses go to college for two reasons. The first is to move up the ol' ladder at work. Become a mine foreman, maybe even superintendent. It's in their blood thick and black as the coal they mine. The second group looks to get the hell outta the mine as quick as they can and go do something else. What that something else is most of 'em haven't got figured out yet. But something else."

"Huh," Mike ponders. "Can't say I'm looking to move up. I'm struggling with things as they are right now."

"I can see that very plainly," the professor offers. "I figured you for one of the ones looking to escape."

"Don't rightly know at this point," Mike offers honestly.

The old professor rises out of his chair and places his hand on Mike's shoulder. "Trust me, young man," he says. "The way you look and the way you're going you won't last long. Them dog holes ain't for everyone. The mines age you. Before you know it, you're prematurely old and broke down, with black lung and living on a pension that ain't worth a dime, that's if the company doesn't screw you outta it."

"So you got out?" Mike asks.

"Damn right I did, and I had a great job. Fire-bossing is an easy gig. Walk the mine all shift, making sure the entries and escape ways are open. Still, wasn't no telling how long it would last. So I went back to school first here, then to Concord and got my master's in business. Teaching don't pay what I made in the mine, but I've been doing this a helluva lot longer than I would've been able to work in the mine. Thirty years now."

Damn, Mike thinks.

Mike studies all weekend for his make-up test. He even calls in sick to work on Monday. The section isn't ready, and he's tired of following Theodore around. That evening, he aces his business course. And he got more outta that class on the last day, just talking with his professor, than he did the entire semester.

Chapter 27

The Greeks worshipped all sorts of gods. It seemed the old Greek gods were quite human in many respects, freely giving of their favor to some and then denying those same favors to others. In modern times, if is often said the Lord giveth and the Lord taketh away. The same must be true of the mine gods, for just as quickly as Mike's crew experiences a record run, it seems the section is beset with calamity, first the water spout, then the conveyor belt breaking, stopping production one day, followed by a flat on a shuttle car halving production another, and finally on this day, the continuous miner blowing a gathering arm motor, the replacement had to be trucked in from the manufacturer's main warehouse in Pennsylvania.

Theodore is beside himself with these malfunctions. For all his bellowing about production, there is little anyone can do about these setbacks. As is normal operating procedures when a section is shut down, the crew is broken up and sent to the four corners of the mine, used as fill in operators for absent workmen on other sections. But even in downtime, there is plenty of work to be done on Mike's section. He is left with only three of his crew to perform all those odd jobs needing to be done, but there is never time to complete, probably as it would be in any manufacturing plant. Mike, Kate, Reggie, and Randy head for the section, awaiting the replacement motor and with instructions to tidy up the place as best they can.

Downtime is a welcome respite for the crew. It is a day where the normal pressures of production can be set aside if only for a short while, and the crew can work at a leisurely pace knowing that whatever work they are going to do will shortly be undone when the section returns to mining coal. Randy and Reggie are to remove the old motor and get ready for the replacement, leaving Mike and Kate do the section scut work: repairing ventilation, rock dusting the entire section, tidying up the dinner hole, organizing the section supplies, and whatever other busy work Theodore can come up with for eight hours.

Randy is a topnotch electrician. He rips the old motor out in short order, and the crew loads it into the scoop. Kate and Mike take the dysfunctional motor to the end of the track and wait for the replacement to arrive. It gives the two an opportunity to talk, a luxury not often afforded during a normal day's run, and Mike the opportunity to find out more about this unique woman. She sits in the cab of the scoop while Mike rests on a half-empty flat car of rock dust. He isn't normally at a loss when it comes to talking to women, but being alone in the dark with a female coal miner is not his normal comfort zone.

"So, Kate," he stammers, trying to come up with something. "How is it that you're on a miner?"

"What kinda question is that, boss? I work in the mine. Why shouldn't I be?" Her tone is half-defensive, half-kidding. Her response catches him off guard.

"Now, wait a minute. I didn't mean nothing by the question. It's just there ain't a lot of women on these sections, much less running a miner. I was just wondering what made you decide to do that is all."

She shakes her head. "Job came open. I bid and got it. That's all. It's good pay. Got me off the owl shift and off the chain gang." The chain gang, as it is called in the mine, is the general labor crew. Those folks got all the dirty jobs no one else wanted. That was where Mike's friends Singer, Runt, and Pecker started until they got their motormen jobs.

"So which was worse? The owl shift or the chain gang?" Seems like a good question, he thought. And one he'd like to have an answer for, as he'd never spent any time on either.

"Man, that's a good one!" She laughs an easy laugh. "Oh, that's right. You're the chosen one. I darn near forgot. Well, let's see. They both were for shit. I could never get used to midnight shift. It just ain't natural. Sleep during the day, up all night. You spent the entire week getting used to the wacky hours, only to screw up and sleep like a normal person on weekends. Come Sunday night, you're back on the weird hours again. And I tried everything. Aluminum foil over the windows, fan running while I tried to sleep, ear plugs, face mask, everything. Still I couldn't get any rest.

"And the chain gang, well now, that's another thing all by its self. Every shit job there was to do, the chain gang got it. Shovel out the sump in mud up to your knees? Chain gang. Belt broke? Chain gang. Track behind? Chain gang. Water line frozen on the mainline in the middle of winter? We chipped it open. And the bosses seemed to take pleasure in having us women do the worst of it. The dirtier, the nastier, the filthier the job, well, we women got it. I know they were doing it just to try and run us off. But I ain't runnin'. No, sir. I'm still here." Mike could hear the defiance in her voice. But something she said struck a nerve.

"What the hell is this 'chosen one' bullshit?"

"Oh, come on, boss!" Kate laughs out loud. "You're Theodore's fair-haired boy. Hand-picked from the day you started, so the story goes. You never worked owl shift, never spent any time on the gang. Minute you got your black cap, on to a section you went. Then the minute you got your time in grade, they make you a boss. Day shift even. Folks say you're being groomed to be his right-hand man, maybe even take his place someday."

"I ain't never heard such—"

"Why, of course, you ain't. You think anyone is gonna say it to your face? I mean, everyone knows you're seeing his daughter. You think he's gonna hand this place over to just anyone?"

"Well, it ain't his to hand over," Mike replies defensively.

"You might think so, but I'd bet a dollar to a donut *he* thinks it is. Banner Fuels might own the place, but it's *his* mine. At least in his mind, that is." Mike couldn't argue the point. The old man often referred to the place as his mine. "That old fart has been here his whole life. Folks say it *is* his whole life. You think he's gonna just give it up without no say so?" She might not know Mr. Theodore, but he thinks she has him sized up pretty well. "Nope, you marry that cute little daughter of his, you take over the run of the place. Sounds like you've pretty much got it the way you want it."

Except I never said I wanted it! Mike screams inside. This line of talk makes him uncomfortable, and Kate is forcing him to see things in a way he had never looked at them before. Time to change the subject.

"And what about you, Kate Matthews? You sound a little bitter."

"Bitter?" she spits the words between her teeth. Then she thinks. "Bitter? Well, maybe I am a little. I've put up with a lot of bullshit here. I've had to fight and claw for everything I got. Even the damn union is against me. They made the company recount the bids on this miner job, to make sure I was the winner. They couldn't believe a woman could get the job, much less do the job."

"And you are damn good at it, Kate."

"You're damn right I am. I have to be. See, if'n I ain't, then all the talk these prejudiced bastards say about women in the mines will be true. That we don't belong here. Most of 'em can't stand us being down here in the first place." Mike begrudgingly knew that was true. It wasn't that many years ago it was considered bad luck for a woman to even be on the property, much less working in the hole.

"Sounds like you don't care for coal miners much," he says only half-jokingly.

"I got little reason to. Was married to one for four years. Got married my senior year in high school. Old sonofabitch was a long-wall plow operator, drank like a fish, and beat the shit out of me nearly every evening. I finally had enough and left him, and that's what led me to the mines. I figured if he could do it, well, I damn sure could."

"You got any kids, Kate?"

"No, thank God. I didn't want to continue his gene pool!" She laughs again, but then her look turns sad. "I was pregnant once, but he beat it outta me," she says lowly. "Probably for the best. No ties, you know?"

"So got you a fella now?" he asks. He immediately regrets asking the question.

"No. You lookin'?" she kids him. "Nope. Just me and my dog. I ain't dated in a while, and I don't date anyone from the mine."

"So you really do have something against coal miners."

"Beside the fact that my ex was one, I reckon that would be enough. But that ain't the reason. I hired in with five women. Each and every one of 'em wound up foolin' around with someone here. A few of 'em broke up a marriage or two themselves. And ain't none of 'em with any of the fellers they were carryin' on with. And lord, you oughta hear how these men talk bad about those gals now! So I figured it best that I just mind my own business and keep things separate as best I can."

"That sounds like a good plan." He agreed that it was best not to give these sharks any extra ammo. Most of them could invent enough gossip on their own. They're not above making stuff up if it makes for a good story.

She shrugs. "It works for me, anyway. How 'bout you, boss man? You fixin' to tie the knot with little Ms. Theodore anytime soon?" Boy, was he so not ready to have this conversation with anyone, much less someone from his crew, and a female member of his crew at that. For some reason, this woman was able to get to the heart of matters rapidly, and it unsettles him.

"I haven't given it much thought," he replies shortly. Which is true. He hasn't.

"Well, you better. Time's a-wastin', and she ain't gonna wait forever, you know."

"What are you, my damn mother?" he chides. In fact, the two are the same age.

Kate laughs an easy laugh. "Man, you really don't know women. It really is like that saying . . ."

"Saying?"

"Yeah, you know, men from some planet, women from another. Your gal is back home from college now, settlin' in. Gonna want to nest before long."

"You nesting?"

"Yep, if you wanna call a two-bedroom trailer up Edmore Holler nesting. Your gal will want more'n that."

"All I got is a one-bedroom apartment downtown in the Tower."

She shakes her head. "That won't do. You'll have to get a sho' enough real house with a nice little yard for all those crumb crushers that will come." She laughs lightly. "Throw in a white picket fence and you've got the whole picture!" For some reason, that picture doesn't fit in Mike's mind.

"Oh, shit," he mumbles.

"Come on, boss!" she cajoles. "That's everyone's dream, ain't it?"

"Is it yours?" he asks.

She is quiet for a moment. "Well, it could be, if it were with the right person. I think that's all any of us are really looking for, ain't it? Someone to love us for who we are, not what they think we should be or what they want us to be." Her face becomes blank. "I think my ex used to beat me not because of who I was, but because of who I wasn't. I wasn't his mother, who always done everything right in the house. I wasn't his drinking buddies, who he spent more time with than he did me. I wasn't his first love, whoever the hell she was, but he spent hours when he was drunk telling me all about her. I was just me, and I don't think that was ever enough for him. In the end, I had to be enough for me. But I think everyone wants someone to love them for them. The way they are has to be enough. If that person was to ever come along, then, yeah, I could live that dream too. We ain't meant to be alone, Mike Thomas."

She called him by his name. Not boss. Not Snake. And that was most unsettling. *Maybe what she says is true, but I'm not at that point yet in my life,* he thinks. Too many things unsettled. He was thankful there were lights in the distance, the motor crew bringing the replacement motor to the section. Tomorrow would be business as usual. Thank God. He really didn't like having this conversation on the best of occasions, and especially not here with her.

Chapter 28

The run complete after pulling a double shift on a Friday night, Mike's crew decides to head for a local watering hole to spend some of their paycheck and let off a little steam.

"You comin', boss man?" Lou asks as the crew exits the cage.

Mike thinks for a minute. Nothing else shaking in McDowell County on a Friday night. "Yeah, I'll head up once I finish my paperwork." He rolls into the lounge on Premier Mountain at 1:00 a.m. The place hasn't changed since his last trip here. He wonders if it ever has, or ever will. A broken down pool table in one corner, the felt surface now a dingy brown, a low-hanging dim bar light over its center. The bar is to the left as you enter the door. There is no draft beer served here— only bottles and cans. The bandstand is to the right, still behind the floor-to-ceiling chicken wire. The country cover band has just finished their final set for the night, and most of the drunken crowd is filing out. The remaining patrons are all pretty well wasted, and Mike notices two men passed out at a table off to the far side of the dance floor. The jukebox has replaced the band in supplying loud noise for the place, cranking out an old country staple that Mike is certain will send anyone who is predisposed to—but isn't already—crying in their beer.

His crewmen are all huddled around the pool table, shooting eight ball and trying to make up for lost drinking time. Mike joins his crew at the table.

"Who's winning?" he asks, twisting the cap off a Stroh's longneck bottle.

"Lou and I won the first one," Mitch the buggy operator says. "But Electro and Gary are kicking our ass in this one."

Mike looks around. Lou, looking at his boss as he tugs on his beer, notices.

"She ain't here, boss man."

"Who ain't here?"

"Don't gimme that shit." Lou grins, as he directs his boss toward two rickety folding chairs they collapse into. "Kate was invited, but she begged off. Said she had to get up early tomorrow to take her mom shopping up in Beckley."

"Well, that'd be an all-day trip."

"Sho'nuff. Roads to Beckley are a damn might more crooked than fifty-two to Bluefield."

"I ain't never been to Beckley," Gary jumps in.

"Hell, have you ever been outside McDowell County, Gary?" Electro asks loudly over the wail of the jukebox.

"Nope. Don't reckon I have. Figure I can get everything I need at the company store in Capels. Except for beer! And there's all kinda places in county for that."

"'Cept on Sunday," Mike chimes in.

"Hell, Snake, that ain't no problem if'n you know where to look."

"That's true," Lou says, rising to take his turn at the pool table. "Reckon it's like most anything. You can find it if you know where to look and are willing to pay for it!"

"'Cept pussy!" Electro howls.

"Oh, hell no," Gary roars back. "There's plenty of places to buy pussy in county. Them gals up Carswell Holler been sellin' it for as long as I've known what it was."

"Reckon you've dropped many a paycheck up that holler then, huh, Gary?" Electro chides.

"Oh, hell naw!" Gary shoots back. "I ain't never paid for no pussy in my life."

"Bullshit!" Mitch joins in. "When you was a child, you was so damn ugly yo' mama had to tie a steak around your neck to get the dog to play with you!" The men roar.

"That may have been so, but now I got a dick the size of your arm. I ain't got no problems with the women with this!" Gary says

134

as he grabs his crotch. The men laugh so hard beer shoots out their noses.

Mike finishes his beer and looks around the bar. At two in the morning, there are still a few women here, but all of 'em look like they're been rode hard and put up wet a few times too many. There might be one or two worth the effort, but he just doesn't feel like trying.

"Fellas, it's late and I'm whipped. I'll see y'all Monday."

"Aw, now, come on, boss man, one game," Electro says. "I ain't never seen you shoot."

Mike relents at the men's insistence. "All right, one game."

"Rack 'em, Gary," Lou calls out. "Boss man and I against any two of you fuckers. Boss man, you break. Losers buy the next round."

Mike picks out a cue stick and chalks it up. He bends over the table and, eyeing the rack, draws the stick back and strikes the cue ball with all he's got. If you can't finesse it, overpower it. The rack breaks with a mighty crack. The balls scatter with explosive speed, scattering all over the table. The eight ball rolls as if guided by a hand to the corner pocket. Game over.

The men roar with laughter.

"Well, screw me blind and call me Shorty," Mitch yelps. "Our boss is the luckiest sumbitch I know."

"Better lucky than good," Lou grins. "Y'all pony up."

"Hell no!" Gary protests. "That was one lucky shot, that's all! I ain't buyin' lest I git beat fair and square."

Mike shakes his head. He used to shoot a lot of pool in old man Theodore's basement when he and Jennifer were in high school, but he was never very good at it.

"Gary's right. It was a lucky shot. Hell, I'll buy you guys this round. Line 'em up, barkeep!" Mike yells to the gap-toothed old man behind the counter.

The men immediately toss their pool sticks on the table and belly up to the bar. Free beer is not something the men are used to, and especially not a round bought by their boss. Mike pays for the round and heads for the door.

"Headin' out, boss man?" Lou asks.

"Yep. I said one game."

"That you did. Thanks for the beer. See ya Monday."

"That'll work."

Mike jumps in his Mustang and fires up the engine. The twin carburetors cause the powerful machine to lurch in idle, like a large cat waiting to pounce. It was good to hang out with the crew, even if only for a short while. Letting the men see their boss outside the mine, letting them get to know you as more than just their hard-ass boss, his father always said was a key to winning their respect.

Kate wasn't here. He was half hoping she would be. Still, seeing her is a dangerous line he dares not cross. Not if he doesn't want to lose his crew. Not if he doesn't want to lose himself.

Chapter 29

The phone rings.

Mike stirs, rolls over, and looks at the clock. Two o'clock in the morning. Through a Jack Daniels-induced fog he fumbles in the darkness for the phone, knocking his Mickey Mouse telephone to the floor. He finds the receiver and raises it to his ear. He offers a sleepy hello.

"Thomas. RT Theodore. Need you to come to the mine, son." The old man's voice sounds like he is regularly up at two in the morning.

"Yes, sir," Mike mumbles, his eyes still closed. "What's going on?"

"Double fatality on evening shift. Roof fall on Wildcat's section. Gonna need men to escort the feds around. Some are already here, more on the way. Get here as quick as you can."

Mike sits straight up. "I'll be right there."

The union parking lot is empty, but the foreman's lot is packed with government vehicles. Mike makes his way past the foreman's office, which is full of mine inspectors, and Theodore is standing in front of the group, pointing at the mine map. Mike walks up to Cal Ripley in the foreman's bathhouse. Cal is the senior day shift foreman, number two in the chain of command under Mr. Theodore, if there ever could be a number two under Mr. Theodore.

"So, Cal, what happened, man?"

"Roof fall on Wildcat's section around nine o'clock. Big one. The entire miner is covered. I hear you can't see anything but the boom. Men have called out to the miner crew, but if that's the case, there ain't no way anyone could've survived that fall."

"Oh, damn."

"That ain't the worst of it. Leadfoot said they were a good thirty feet beyond the last row of roof bolts. Said he'd flagged 'em to stop and back out more than once, but they kept cutting. Then the place just fell in."

Mike's knees weaken, and he collapses on the bench. That was his old crew. He knew full well that Polecat was notorious for mining beyond the pins, more often than not simply because he didn't want to move the miner. Stinky was all too willing to go along with it, because most of the work moving the miner fell on him. And Wildcat begrudgingly went along, not wanting to upset his men.

"Where is Wildcat?"

"He's still on the section, along with the rest of the crew working to get the men out. The owl shift was sent home before they ever went underground. One owl shift crew was sent to relieve the evening shift crew who were moved over to the section to help, but Wildcat's crew is still there. The rest of the mine is empty, except for the fire bosses making their rounds."

Closing a mine is normal procedure following a fatality. Production won't resume until the feds release the mine, and that could take a while. Theodore limps into the bathhouse. His face looks even more worn than usual.

"Cal, you and Thomas take these inspectors down to the section. Just got off the phone with the section, and they're gettin' close to the miner cab. Get the bodies out, then get everyone off the section." Mike found what Theodore said telling. It was obvious to him, and everyone present, there was little hope for the two men. "Cal, assist the inspectors as best you can. Whatever they need, give it to 'em."

Once dressed, the two foremen head to the cage. The inspectors are there, dressed in their trademark striped reflective overalls. The lead inspector removes a red tag from his vest pocket and wires it to the cage door. More symbolic than meaningful, a mine that is "red tagged" is closed to production until the mine inspector deems the mine safe to resume production and removes the tag. The trip to the section is quiet. The foremen do not talk to the inspectors, and the inspectors do not talk among themselves. Arriving at the end of the track, the group proceeds directly up the track entry to the site of the fall. There are twenty men in a bucket line, handing rock one at a time, trying to clear a path to the miner cab. Mike looks up the entry through a narrow tunnel hacked in the rock to near the back of the cab. Wildcat is at the head of the line, digging frantically with a pickaxe, his enormous arms flailing away at the rock, crying out with each stroke for the two men. Mike places his hand on the shoulder of the last man in the line, Skank, who jumps wildly. He settles down when he recognizes his old crewmate.

"How ya holdin' up, Skank?" Mike asks softly.

"It's bad, Snake. It's bad." Skank drops his head. "Damn fools. Leadfoot tried to get 'em to pull out. Raceway too. They just kept goin'. Then the whole place just fell. No warning at all. No popping of the top, no creaks, no groans, it just fell. Sounded like the whole mountain had come down on 'em. Dust everywhere. Couldn't see for what seemed like forever. Leadfoot backed out so quick he rammed his car into the opposite wall and cut all the machine cables. Can't even bring the pinner over to shore up the area. Got some jacks set to prop up the roof, and a few in there holding up the rock as we tunneled in." He drops on all fours to the mine floor, breathing hard. "Wildcat has been at it nonstop since the roof fell. His heart is going to explode. The man can't keep going like this."

Mike looks back at Cal and the inspectors. To their credit, the feds look at the ongoing work from a distance, content that all is being done as safely as it could be to free the workmen from their trap. Their job will start later. Mike edges past the men in the line to the head of the narrow tunnel carved out of the rock. The stale air is full of the odor of sweat and shit and vomit. Edging beside Wildcat, he stops the burly man swinging the pickaxe.

"Hey, boss, let me spell ya here," he says softly to the miner. "You need a break."

"No, brother. I gotta get my men outta here. I gotta do it," he says frantically. Sweat drips from his bearded face, and Mike sees the blood dripping from the tips of every one of his fingers. The man has literally clawed his way through the rock to the back of the operator's cab. "Polecat!" he cries out again. "Stinky! Can you hear me, boys? I'm almost to ya!" There is no reply.

"Hey, brother," Mike says again, even softer. "Step out. Give a fresh man a turn. Go get you some water. Then come back."

Wildcat stops his picking. He turns and looks at Mike. The man's face is covered with black grime, blood, and streaked with tears. Sweat runs like a river from the tip of his dark beard, and Mike can see the crazed madness in his eyes. He grasps the pickaxe from the man, pats him on the shoulder as he motions him to go to the rear. Wildcat moves off.

Mike picks for just a few moments when he finally pushes through to the rear of the cab. Removing his hard hat, he shines the beam of light into the small dark opening. The metal canopy has collapsed vertically from the weight of the rock, compacting the canopy down onto the large metal electrical control box into an area only eighteen inches in height. In this small area is the miner operator. The man is lurched forward, mashed between the top of the canopy and the forward control panel. His torso is pressed down, way down between his knees. His head is turned awkwardly too far to the left, his cap light is crushed and blood is dripping from his nose and mouth and running from his ear. Mike reaches through the opening and nudges the miner. No movement. He looks to the right, out the opening of the canopy. He sees a hand rising from the floor and resting on the operator's boot, and with his light follows the arm until it completely disappears under a solid wall of rock. Mike drops his head. Putting his hard hat back on, he turns to the man behind him.

"Pass the word. They're both gone."

Chapter 30

It takes another twelve hours to free the bodies. The rest of Wildcat's crew leaves after the fate of the men is determined. Wildcat stays until they are freed and rides out with the bodies. Their mangled corpses are placed in a man bus, covered with a tarp and transported outside, where an ambulance is waiting and the bodies are taken to the local hospital, then to the morgue.

While a fresh crew begins the work of uncovering the mining machine, the mine safety and health administration inspectors begin their investigation. Every man on the section is interviewed at length, but the most intense questioning is reserved for Wildcat. It is widely known before the bodies are recovered that the crew had committed a major violation of mining laws by proceeding beyond safe limits, and the crew had paid for it with their life. Now it was Wildcat's turn to pay with a pound of his flesh. After all, everything that occurs on a working section is ultimately the section foreman's responsibility. Multiple violations are written, which will cost the company thousands of dollars in fines, not to mention the lost production during a lengthy federal investigation.

As is standard operating procedure in a multiple fatality, MSHA does not limit their investigation to the area of the incident. The entire mine is inspected with a fine-tooth comb, resulting in even more citations, more fines, and further lost production. For three days the entire mine work force is devoted to correcting the violations without a pound of coal produced. The mine is still under a red tag, and Theodore pushes everyone to correct the violations as quickly as possible to get the closure order lifted. Everyone goes about their business somberly as instructed, but everyone silently knows the order will not be lifted until the miner is recovered, the entry pinned up and secured, and a thorough detailed investigation of the accident site is conducted.

The process becomes political at some point. A member of the union safety committee is allowed to accompany each federal mine inspector on his rounds, and many of them use this opportunity to point out as many safety violations as they can find. Under normal circumstances, some of the mine inspectors would use their common sense and good judgment as to whether these minor violations warranted a citation, but under the current situation, every possible violation is cited to the fullest extent the law allows. The union safety officials from the district office come for their own separate investigation, then make their customary statement to the local papers about the company making willful violations of mining safety laws, its total lack of regard for worker safety, and that the union will always be the only stalwart for worker safety. Then they get in their company cars and retreat to the comfort of their air-conditioned offices. But not before making it clear that Wildcat was going to pay. Union pressure, which is considerable, is brought to bear on the local law enforcement authorities, and there is talk that Wildcat will face criminal charges. A coal mine runs on rumor, and words are tossed around the bathhouse. Manslaughter. Negligent homicide.

The foreman is brought in for yet another round of interrogation. Pointed questions are asked for which he has no good answers. After all, the crew did commit serious safety violations. When the entry is cleared, it is determined the miner cab was forty feet beyond the last row of roof bolts. Forty feet! Two full cuts. No way on earth anyone could justify that, and Wildcat does not even try. Theodore sends the man home, suspended with pay, until the firestorm dies down.

The funeral of the two miners is well attended, the pews packed to overflowing, with the unusual sight of news trucks parked outside the churches. The small town is used to coal mine deaths, but a double fatality is a rarity and casts a heavier pall than usual. There are also folks outside the church with makeshift signs condemning the company, which plays well for the television cameras. Both coffins are closed, and while the rest of the crew attend the services, Wildcat, on Theodore's advice, stays away. Jennifer goes with Mike to both services, dressed in her best Sunday outfit from the specialty women's store in Charleston, her blond hair cropped short and turned up at the end. She looks every bit the cheerleader she did in high school. Kate is also there, and she and Mike exchange glances during the service. Kate is dressed plainly in a mid-length button up dress, fresh off the rack at JC Penny, her red hair down around her shoulders. She has a fresh-scrubbed look and wears no make-up, yet Mike is struck by her simple beauty.

After four days, the mine inspectors, having covered every square inch of the underground workings and the preparation plant for good measure, lifts the closure order. The mine may resume production. But there is one big question for Theodore to answer. Who will run this miner, and who will run this crew? Miners are a superstitious lot by nature, and even though it is a different machine, the original one destroyed by the fall, no one wants to be the man to crawl back into that cab. Even more important, who will be the man to lead this crew? Theodore knows that it will be a long time, if ever, before Wildcat returns to the working face. Despite the serious talk the man has committed major errors, and even if he is somehow cleared, crews will be reluctant to work under him again. Mike Thomas volunteers for the duty, which both surprises and pleases Theodore, yet he denies his request out of hand. He is too close to this crew, and too green to handle this situation. Plus, he's decided to move Mike's dad to that section to be the miner helper. He is the most senior man in that job category on the second shift, and while Theodore doesn't necessarily care for some of Mr. Thomas's union views, he knows the man will always do his job the right way. Mr. Thomas won't stand for any unsafe nonsense. As for the miner operator, the rock crew operator will do for now, until the job is filled by bid. Everyone in the mine will know where the opening is, and Theodore figures anyone bidding on the job will know where he's going and what he's getting himself into. He decides to place Cal Ripley on the crew, if only for a short while, until things quiet down. Cal has a steady hand, and the men will respect him and follow him.

And he too won't put up with any nonsense. Production throughout the mine will be slow for a while, as men take their time and exhibit extreme caution in their jobs until their nerves settle. Theodore also knows that even though the closure order is lifted, mine inspectors will be a constant presence in the mine, visiting every working section on every shift in the immediate future. The men will be on their best behavior whenever the law is around. Perhaps in a month, maybe longer, operations will return to normal. Until then, it will be all they can do to muddle through and mine what coal they can.

Just when it seems the mine is ready to ramp back up and things return to normal, the entire place is shaken to its core by another blow. Unable to deal with the grief of losing two men under his charge, Wildcat Hatfield put his .450 Marlin hunting rifle to another use, and the life it claimed this time was his own. The roof fall on his section has taken yet another life.

Chapter 31

The death of the workers and Wildcat's suicide casts a new shadow over the mine. Morale falls to a new low and absenteeism soars. On many shifts, the foremen struggle to fill a third of the production crews. Old man Theodore, in a rare show of understanding, decides to let his foremen take some days off. No one needs the time off more than Mike. The deaths have hit him hard, and he has trouble sleeping, which even the Jack Daniels can't fix.

Jennifer notices the change in his demeanor. The closeness that had been growing between them has taken a downturn, and she knows between his work and going to school, he has little spare time for the two of them. She hopes the time away will give him a chance to decompress and for them to reconnect.

It is a short four-hour interstate drive south from the West Virginia hills to the Great Smoky Mountains, a favorite honeymoon destination for hillbilly newlyweds. The resort area is packed with wedding chapels, motels touting heart-shaped hot tubs and in-room fireplaces, and fine dining establishments dot the parkway.

The young couple chooses a lodge squarely in midtown Gatlinburg, and their walks along the parkway in and out of the little fudge shops and tourist traps improves Mike's disposition. After a hike up to Clingman's Dome and dinner the second night at a local trout house over fried mountain trout and a bottle of Riesling, Mike begins to loosen up.

"Thanks for suggesting this trip, Jen. It was good to get away."

She grins. "You've had a lot to deal with the last little bit." She reaches across the table and squeezes his hand.

"No more than anyone else. At least I'm able to get away. Wildcat and his men won't be doing that anymore."

"It's a tragedy, that's for sure." She doesn't know what else to say.

"A tragedy? Is that what you think it was?" he asks as he takes a large gulp of wine.

"Why, sure. The death of three men in the prime of life. I think that's tragic. Don't you?"

"Their death is tragic, no doubt of that. The real tragedy though is that none of it had to happen."

"Mike, working in the mine carries its risks. Everyone who goes down there knows that and accepts it."

"Hell, I know that. I've been doing this for long enough to know the dangers inherent with this damn job. This job's dangerous enough on its own. It's when you get lazy and stretch safety margins when you're asking for trouble . . . risking your life."

"So what are you saying? Is that what happened here? Dad said the men were killed in a roof fall."

"Well, yeah, that's the official story. What the paper reported is what the mine officials put out there for public consumption. What the paper didn't report but what really happened was that those guys were really pushing it, mining way beyond the roof bolts. And it was simply because they were too damn lazy to take the time to move the miner to another place and Wildcat didn't want to piss 'em off by making 'em move."

"That's awfully cold, Mike," Jennifer says softly, looking down at her plate.

"Well, it might be cold but it's the truth. I worked on that section for damn near three years. I know." Mike takes another large gulp of the sweet white wine. "You know, this ain't half bad stuff. Beats the hell outta Stroh's."

"So, you're being careful, aren't you?" she asks earnestly.

"As careful as a man can be down there, I reckon," he answers, picking at the flaky white fish. "I ain't gonna take any unnecessary risks, that's for sure. None of my men are gonna pull any crazy stunts like Wildcat's crew. Not that they would anyway. And especially now, what with the feds crawling all over the place like stink on shit. But soon they'll be gone, and the place will return to normal, and someone will get tired and take shortcuts, and it will happen again. Bet on it."

"That's a rather pessimistic view, I think," she offers, concern showing in her eyes.

"Yeah, well, I call it realistic," he replies. "It's the nature of the business."

"Sounds like you aren't real happy with the business."

"I'm not. I think it might be time for a change."

"Really?" she asks, feigning surprise. "What do you want to do?"

"I don't know right off," he says. "But I got options now. My degree came in the mail the other day."

"You graduated?" Jen interrupts excitedly. "That's fantastic! Why didn't you tell me? That's a reason to celebrate right there!"

"You're right." Mike smiles. "I suppose it is. Picking it up at the post office with bills and other junk mail takes some of the luster off it though, you know? Still, the only thing I could think of sitting there looking at the sheepskin was, what's next?"

"Well, that's a question I think all of us have after graduation. You're in a different place than many though. While most graduates have to think about a job after graduation, you already have a job. The degree will help you move up at the mine."

"But what if I don't want to move up at the mine? What if this isn't the job I want, Jen? Heck, what if this isn't the life I want? I mean, is this all there is here? I get to mine coal, do the same thing day in and day out for the rest of my life? One day after another for the next forty years until I'm old and broke down with nothing to show for it but a meager pension and an oxygen tank? That doesn't sound very appealing to me. Is this the life you want?"

"Yeah, I'm happy here." She sits up in her chair and looks at him. "I went away to school and I'm happy to be back home and in my classroom and teaching my kids. My support system is here. One thing I missed about college was my family support system. You know, being able to sit down at the dinner table and talk with Mom and Dad. But I'm not finished. I'd like to settle down and start a family. Remember me telling you my grandma's saying: 'Child, don't you get you no man till you don't need you no man.' Well, I don't need no man now, so I think I might like to get one." She gives him a faint smile.

"Maybe that's it. I've never been anywhere but here," he replies. "I don't think working in the mine is for me long term. I've got my degree now. I've been thinking a lot lately about leaving. Going somewhere away from the hills and these coal mines. Go somewhere where they don't even know what a coal mine is. I want to enjoy what I do, have a passion for it. I want it to be more than a job, Jen."

"Wow, that's a leap." Tears well in her eyes. "What about a family, Mike? No plans for that?" The conversation hasn't gone in the direction she thought it was heading when it started.

"I think I would like a family sometime too, sure, but not here. I don't want the coal mines to be my children's legacy as it was mine from my father. Hell, Jen, you know there ain't nothing else for folks in these hills. You're either a coal miner, or a doctor treating their black lung, or their lawyer trying to get them their benefits, or a teacher teaching miner's kids. I may make less money outside the dog hole, but I won't have to take chances with my life to make a living! You gotta take too many risks in the mine to produce. I ain't gonna do it. I have to sleep at night. I am not gonna wind up like Wildcat!"

"This is how you feel?"

"Yep. It's like that. I just don't think there is any future for me here. Don't you ever think about going somewhere else?"

"I've been somewhere else," she replies sharply. "I don't wanna be anywhere else. This is my home. My family is here. So is yours. I hoped we would make a life for us here too."

"I care for you, Jen. I really do. But I have never led you on, have I?"

"No, you have not," she answers bluntly, throwing her napkin onto the table. "I had hoped we would build a life together. Convinced myself that was true. You have never given me any reason to think that might come to be, but still I hoped. I see now that probably isn't going to happen." Tears fall from her face into her plate. "Please take me home."

It is a silent four-hour ride back to the West Virginia hills. No words pass between them the entire drive.

Chapter 32

Mike returns to the mine a few days early. The crew is surprised to see him back so soon, but none ask him the reason for his quick return.

After their shift one Friday night, Mike agrees to join the crew for a beer at a local watering hole in Bluefield. It's eight o'clock in the evening by the time he arrives, and the rest of the crew have commandeered a large table in the corner and are already well oiled. Several pitchers of Stroh's are on the table, and Mike pours himself a glass, quickly kills it, and pours himself another.

"Good shit, ain't it?" Mitch says, talking a swig off his beer and a drag off his cigarette. "The band ain't half bad either. Playing a lot of George Jones and Hank Williams tunes. Right up my alley, man!"

The bar is like most any other. Smoke filled, flashing neon lights over the bar advertising the available beers, a small dance area in front of the bandstand, which, unlike those in McDowell County, isn't separated from the band with floor-to-ceiling chicken wire. Mike settles into a folding chair and sips his beer.

"So, Snake, enjoyin' yourself?" He looks up to see Kate looking down at him. She is dressed in a sleeveless dress that clings to her body in all the right places, and the high heels she's wearing makes her taller and lither. Her red hair drapes down on her shoulders, and she has a nice brown tan that isn't evident in her bib overall work clothes.

"I am now," he answers, rising to his feet and, rounding the table, pulls out her chair. "I didn't think you'd make it down tonight."

"Ah, hell, a girl's gotta let her hair down every once in a while." She smiles at him.

"Mitch says the band is good."

"I reckon." She shrugs. "Hank and George ain't my favorites, but these fellas make it sound better than I recall. Or maybe it's just because it's loud!"

"One way to cover a bad band is by cranking up the volume. It's not my taste either. I just came for the beer," he offers with a smile.

"Well, finish that one off. You and I are gonna dance." She grabs his arm and jerks him to his feet.

Mike takes her hand and she leads him to the dance floor. The band is starting another set and their first song is a slow rendition of "Smoky Mountain Memories." Kate turns and throws her arms around Mike's neck, and the two begin to sway slowly to the music. Mike isn't much of a dancer, and his feet appear glued to the floor. Kate doesn't seem to mind, and the two just stand in the center of the dance floor, swaying to the music.

"So, do this a lot, do you?" Kate says teasingly. Already self-conscious, Mike's face reddens.

"You enjoy teasing me, Kate?"

"Well, yeah. A little. You're such an easy target."

"You kid with all the guys at work. I notice. But you seem to take a special pleasure at getting my goat."

"Bother you, does it?" she asks, her arms tightening behind his neck.

"Nah, not really," he lies. "I reckon it's just your way."

She laughs lightly. "A girl's gotta keep her guard up around all those wolves. It's either pick at 'em a little or cuss 'em till a fly wouldn't light on 'em. That wouldn't be good. Hard enough getting these fellas to accept ya. In my case, best I can hope for is to be tolerated. At least on our section, the guys don't flirt or aren't crass. Anymore anyway."

"Oh yeah? They used to hit on you?"

"Man, are you kidding? There wasn't a day when I started underground that someone didn't. The miners were bad. The bosses were worse. Complaining done no good. I saw what happened to some of the other gals who bitched."

"Oh, yeah?"

"Cold shoulder from everyone after that. You gotta have some-one watching your back down there. Without a buddy, you're in a bad way. And then I saw a few other women take up with a man. Every one of those ended badly, and then the way they were treated was even worse than the one who complained. Figured my best defense was a good offense. Give 'em hell, in a nice way. It's worked so far."

Mike smiles. This is one sharp lady. And tough.

"Don't ya think we're giving 'em something to wag their tongues about come Monday?" she asks.

"Reckon so," he nods. "Don't cha think that'll hurt your tough girl image, Kate?"

She shakes her head. "Nah. What the hell. As long as I don't leave the place with ya, I figure I'm safe."

"Well, damn. And that was just what I was planning," Mike kids, only half-jokingly. It is Kate's turn to blush.

"Besides, you got the princess to keep you warm at night," she teases. The mention of Jennifer causes him to tense up, and with their closeness, Kate notices. The song ends, and Mike walks away from her back to the table. Kate follows him.

"I'm sorry," she offers. "Sometimes I get carried away and prob-ably say things I shouldn't. If I struck a nerve, I apologize."

Mike sees the sincerity in her gaze. "Nah, it ain't you. It's all on me. The 'princess' as you call her and I aren't seein' much of each other these days." Mike pours himself another mug and offers to refill Kate's glass. She shakes her head. "I'd better not. It's a long drive from here back to Edmore, and the police will be out at this hour."

"Suit yourself." Mike throws down the draft beer in two gulps and refills his glass.

"So anything you wanna talk about?" She sits in the chair beside him. He thinks for a minute and is about to tell her about it all when Dave, the roof bolter, comes up to the table.

"Hey, doll, how about a dance?" he asks her through a buck-toothed grin, slurring his words.

"Reckon you can, Dave? I do believe you're about to fall down."

"Maybe so. Then I reckon one dance is all I got left." Kate looks at Mike. Her eyes say I'll stay, but Mike smiles and gives her a knowing nod. "I'll be back in a flash." She turns to Dave. "One dance, Dave, and if it's a slow one, you damn well better keep your hands to yourself."

"Yes'm," Dave slurs and does a bend at the waist, almost falling down with the effort. Thankfully the band cuts loose a stirring rendition of "Sweet Home Alabama," allowing the two to keep a safe distance apart, except when Kate has to reach out and steady him. The song done, Kate quickly returns to the table.

"You handled that well, Kate." Mike tips his beer glass to her.

"Ah, twern't nothing," Kate replies. "Figure I know how to handle coal miners by now."

"That's probably true."

"Oh, no doubt. Guys like Dave ain't no trouble. All bark. He's harmless. It's the quiet ones you have to watch. You know the sayin'. Still waters run deep. You know. Guys like you."

His turn to blush again. "Hell, I'm harmless too, Kate."

"Harmless! Not in this lifetime. Guys like you are dangerous. Break a gal's heart without even tryin'. I bet there are layers to you ain't no one seen yet."

"Not me. I'm an open book. What you see is what you get."

"I call bullshit on that one. There's more to you than what one sees. I'd bet on it."

"And I'm sure the same can be said of you, Kate. All tough on the outside, but there's something about you too."

Kate leans in close. "I'm more woman than you can handle," she whispers. "You can bet on that. But you gotta get to know me first. That's my rule."

"Roger that. Didn't figure you for a one-night stand kinda gal at all, Kate," Mike says softly.

"I have a great urge to plant one on those cute lips," she coos. "But I reckon we've given the crew enough to gossip about. See you Monday." She grabs her bag and heads out the door.

Mike looks down into his glass, trying hard not to watch her leave. He fails, looking at her sashay out the door. Damn, if she doesn't look different outside the hole.

As she clears the door, Dave comes and flops into her empty chair.

"Forget it, boss man. Ain't nothin' there for you."

"No?"

"Naw. Every man at the mine has tried to get at that. She's shot every one of 'em down. And some not too kindly." Dave takes a draw off his cigarette. "That's one cold bitch right there. Some folks think she's a dyke."

I ain't believing that shit, Mike thinks. She didn't give off that vibe.

"That's why most of 'em have slap give up," Dave continues. "Figure there's no use. But not me, no, sir. Sooner or later I nail 'em all!" He laughs drunkenly.

Mike looks around the bar. It's 12:45 a.m., and the place closes in fifteen minutes. However, at a table across the dance floor are two women. Old women. But, like the song goes, if you can't be with the one you love, love the one you're with. He picks up the pitcher and saunters over to their table.

"So, ladies, it's getting late. Want some company?"

Chapter 33

Coal mining has not changed much over the years. Before the advent of mechanized mining when the coal was extracted by hand, the basic layout was the same. The room-and-pillar method of coal extraction is the basic design of coal mines. Even though the volume of coal extracted each shift increased exponentially with the development of mechanized loaders and then continuous miners, both of those developments were based around the time-honored room-and-pillar mining process.

The biggest advancement in mining was longwall mining. The technology promised even larger tonnage per shift than continuous miners deliver, and longwall mining requires a huge commitment of capital and a redesign of mine layout. The longwall is a very apt, descriptive term. The process begins with the development of two parallel conventional room and pillar sections separated by a five-hundred-foot pillar of coal. After mining the sections, or driving the sections ahead for a mile, the sections turn toward each other and intersect, leaving a huge block of coal five hundred feet wide and over a mile long. At the far end of this block, the longwall is installed. The longwall system consists of the shearer, twin drum head ranging arms each equipped with a cutting head rotor, which cuts or shears the coal from the block in three foot slivers. The shearer sits atop a five hundred-foot-long armored face conveyor, which resembles a long sprocket and this is the means the shearer is pulled along the face. The sheared coal falls onto an underlying face conveyor chain, which carries the sheared coal to the conveyor belt, which then transports the coal to the surface. The exposed roof must be supported to protect the miners, and this is accomplished by huge hydraulic jacks called chocks, which are about six feet wide and placed side by side along the entire length of the longwall face. The chocks are connected to the conveyor chain and are pressurized against the mine roof and literally hold the mountain up. As the shearer moves laterally parallel to the face mining coal, the chocks advance the armored face conveyor and chain conveyor forward by hydraulics, then once the conveyors are in place, the chock is lowered from the roof, advances itself forward by hydraulics to the conveyor chain, and then re-pressurized against the roof. As the longwall advances, the exposed roof behind the chocks eventually falls while the workmen remain safe under the pressurized chocks. The entire longwall process resembles a five-hundred-foot-long blacksnake writhing along a wall. The process is continuous in either lateral direction, and the attraction of the process is that none of the support work required for developing a conventional room and pillar section: roof bolting, rock dusting, and downtime transporting the miner from one entry to another, is required. The miners are much safer as they are constantly under the protection of the chock and are not exposed to the unsupported roof as is the case in conventional mining. The longwall is simply a constant, continuous flow of coal.

The mine has been developing the first longwall section or panel as it is termed for a while now. Mike's section has been driving the head gate side of the panel, the side where the track and conveyor belt will be located, while a similar section has been developing the tailgate side of the panel 500 feet away. The mine has been abuzz about the arrival of this new technology, and the miners are all gossiping about the bids for the jobs on this new section. It's been rumored the crew will even be sent to England for a short period to learn how to operate the longwall equipment ahead of it being installed at the Banner Mine.

Old man Theodore is not enamored with the new technology, nor with the strangers, mostly Englishmen, running loose around his mine. Longwall technology was developed in England over 200 years ago and most of the longwall equipment manufacturers are based there. The company has invested well over a million dollars in this equipment, and consultants are everywhere because there is no one at the mine with any experience with this technology. These Englishmen, "limeys" as they are called by the workmen, will teach the crews to operate the machinery.

Theodore has decisions to make. The bids will decide the union workmen who will man the equipment, but he will decide who will be the foremen to oversee "the wall."

These aren't easy decisions. Putting men on the wall means pulling good men off existing sections and disrupting the section chemistry. But he knows that by and large all his section foremen want a shot at this. Cal Ripley is an obvious choice. He's middle-aged, level headed, yet seasoned. He'll be a shift boss someday, and this will be good experience for when that job comes. There is talk from the big office that if this thing is successful, there may be another longwall installed and that means the entire mine will be redesigned and centered around longwall mining. If that happens, experience on the wall will be an absolute must. The third shift will be maintenance, so a production man won't be needed there. That leaves the second shift to be filled. The obvious choice is Mike Thomas. He's young, he's sharp, and he is a good foreman. He's a college graduate now, and while folks underground don't seem to care, the brass knows every boss possessing a college degree. But there's something about him that just doesn't sit well. He and Jennifer aren't seeing each other anymore. Jennifer hasn't spoken about it since it happened over two months ago, choosing to keep whatever passed between them to herself. Mike is working every day, and the section is producing, but he doesn't show the enthusiasm he'd like to see out of his foremen. Then again, he never has. It is as if he is just going through the motions these days. Theodore isn't sure if the issue with Jennifer is the cause, or what it is necessarily, but he doesn't seem to be the same man he once was. And he damn sure ain't putting him on the wall with his current attitude. Maybe if his attitude improves. But not now.

Chapter 34

Having finished another Friday run, the crew moves quicker than normal from the faces to the man bus as it is the end of another work week. It is also a payday Friday and paychecks await the crew topside. Mike always makes a final run across the faces before leaving the section, to ensure all is as it should be for the oncoming shift.

"Hurry the hell up, boss man!" Dave yells from the man bus. "That payday's already burnin' a hole in my pocket and I ain't even got it yet!"

Mike piles into his customary seat in the operator's cab of the man bus. Lou takes it easy to the shaft bottom, much to the chagrin of the crew. Once topside, as the crew washes the thick coal mud from their boots, Kate walks up to her boss.

"You got plans tonight, boss?"

"Nope. Dinner, then zone out in front of the TV. Typical Friday night in the tower."

"Well, we're playin' cards at my place. You're welcome to join us."

"Thanks, Kate, but I don't gamble. One of the few things I learned from my family. I never knew of my dad to gamble money on anything in his life. Money's too hard to come by, he said, to piss it away gambling."

"No, it ain't like that. We're playing Rook."

"Rook? Hell, I'm in."

"Good. We start at seven. You bring the beer and pizza." Mike wonders if he's been invited to play or bring the refreshments. I bet she's heard about the round at the bar.

Pulling into Kate's trailer park, he drives past row upon row of single-wide mobile homes wedged tight against each other, like

157

books in a shelf. He spots Kate's trailer by her little brown Datsun in the driveway. He parks his Mustang behind her car and bounds the three steps to her small deck.

"Come on in, Mike," Kate says politely, holding the vinyl door. Inside at the kitchen table sit Lou, her partner on the mines, and his wife Mary.

"Howdy, boss," Lou calls to Mike. "You got the Stroh's?" Mike holds up a case of longnecks.

"Well, pull up a chair and pop the top on some of those," Mary says, smiling at Mike. "You know how to play this game?"

Rook is a simple four-suit game. Easy to learn how to play, with a number of variations. The preferred variant Mike has played is known as Kentucky discard. The game deck consists of forty-five cards, eleven each in four colors: red, green, yellow, and black, plus one supreme wild card, a crow holding a hand of cards in its wing known as the Rook, which is where the game gets its name. The game is played with two-person teams pitted against each other, each player dealt ten cards with the remaining five cards placed in a pile called the kitty in the center of the table. Each player estimates how many of the total one hundred and eighty points in the deck they can earn in the form of a bid, and the high bid wins the five cards in the kitty, which the bidder then combines with the ten cards in their hand to make the best ten-card hand they can form, discarding the five worst cards from their hand. The bidder then starts play, calling a trump color from his hand. Trump color is supreme, surpassing all other cards of equal or lesser value of a different color. Play proceeds clockwise from the bidder, with the highest number card in the color played winning the turn, unless a trump card is played.

"You get to partner with Kate tonight, Mike," Mary offers. "I can't let Lou and Kate partner up. If they were to lose, you'd never be able to get along with 'em on the section."

"Yeah, this way one of us gets to brag next week." Lou laughs.

Oh great, Mike thinks silently. He really didn't know what to expect coming here tonight. Maybe a group of people playing cards, drinking beer and having a rowdy old time. Instead it is an intimate gathering of four people—two couples—and now he's been partnered for cards with the only other single person here. He'd consider it a set-up, except he walked right into it.

During the first few hands, he sees he's got the better of the partners. Kate plays cards with intensity and has an almost photographic recall of the cards played. While the game is incredibly simple, there is much strategy involved in playing a hand, and Kate demonstrates a master's skill. After three quick games, which Kate and Mike have won decisively, Lou calls for a break. The four adjourn to Kate's small living room, Lou and Mary settling onto the cheap sofa. Kate offers Mike the recliner while she pulls up a kitchen chair.

"Damn, Kate, you're really a card shark." Mike grins. His initial uneasiness has been displaced with the flush of winning.

"Just at this game." Kate smiles shyly. Her red hair shines bright under the incandescent lights overhead. "All my mother's family played Rook. Cutthroat, vengeful, win-at-all-costs Rook players. There were many Saturday nights when my aunts and uncles would congregate at our home, or one of theirs, for all-night Rook marathons. Guys against gals. Husbands against wives. Sisters against brothers-in-law. But never family against family. There'd be hell to pay at home later if one family member made a blunder that resulted in a loss to another family, so it was an unwritten rule that no husband and wife would play another husband and wife. Ever.

"The kitchen would become so cigarette smoke-filled it would put the bawdiest pool hall to shame. The coffee pot perked constantly, and the players became so wired from the coffee and the stress of the games it could get testy early in the wee hours of Sunday morning. Of course, as a child, I was sent to bed early, but fell asleep many nights to the sound of serious gaming going on in the nearby kitchen.

"My mother was the ultimate Rook card shark. The woman could make any bid, no matter how high or what cards were against her. And she could set you if you outbid her, no matter how low your bid, which was a rare occurrence. Mother was a spiteful woman when it came to cards. She wanted to win every game, every hand, and woe be the opponent who stood in her way.

"When I was old enough to earn a place at the card table, it became my mission during the Rook games to beat my mother. The sides were always my father and I versus my mom and sister, 'cause like I said, husband and wife couldn't be on the same team. My dad was a decent Rook player in his own right, but he wasn't the player Mom was. I think he wanted to beat her as badly as I did. But our victories were few and far between. There were games where I knew, I just knew, I had her beat, but she always managed to pull victory away from me. There were a few times when I stood at the table and told her aloud that I had her, I was going to set her ass, but I never did. She had a way with the game. Or maybe she just had a way of intimidating me. After a while, Mom had that effect on Dad and me. But it didn't stop us from trying. I guess I just can't turn it off."

"Damn, woman, no wonder you kicked our asses!" Lou roars.

"So we gonna play again?" Kate asks. She clearly enjoys the game, or maybe it's just the company.

"Naw. Hell, it's almost midnight. Way past my and maw's bedtime. We're headin' out. Ready to go, maw?" Lou motions to his wife, and the two make their way to the door.

"I'd better head out too," Mike jumps up. "I've got mine patrol tomorrow." He does, but not until noon. Kate holds the door for them. "Thanks for comin', y'all," she says as she holds the door for them.

"Thanks for inviting me, Kate," Mike stops to tell her as he stands in the doorway. She wears little makeup, and she doesn't need that. "I had a great time."

"Glad you decided to come. You seemed a little nervous at first, but you loosened up as the night went on."

"It was the beer."

"It'll do that."

"Nah. It was the company."

She smiles. "Well, we'll just have to do it again sometime."

"I'd like that." He has an incredible urge to hold her, and the look in those big green eyes says he can, but he doesn't want to complicate things.

"Be sweet, Kate. See you Monday."

Chapter 35

Living in rural West Virginia in the 1970s was a leap back fifty years in time. There were no convenience stores, no fast-food restaurants, no big box wholesale stores. There were a few drive-in restaurants open until one o'clock in the morning on the weekends, but by the time the evening shift finishes up during the week, the drive-ins are closing down. This presents a dilemma for Mike and Cal Ripley one Friday night, having pulled a double shift and decided to find a late-night greasy spoon.

"Hey, I hear there's a new Huddle House open all night over in Princeton," Cal offers as the two dress in the foreman's bathhouse. "We've got the day off tomorrow. Wanna try it out?"

"Princeton? That's an hour from here."

"That's thirty minutes in your hot rod." Cal laughs.

"Reckon so. I'm in. Let's ride."

They do make the trip in forty minutes. Mike is used to making the run up Highway 52 to Bluefield, and Princeton is only a few miles on down the road. The Huddle House sits like an oasis in the middle of a dark desert, its large neon sign easily seen in the otherwise pitch dark for miles. The Huddle House sits just off the exit of the West Virginia Turnpike. A new large service station is under construction across the parking lot from the diner. Seems civilization is at last coming to this area.

The diner is sparsely populated at two in the morning. A couple, obviously from out of state judging by their floral summer shirts and dark tans, occupy the end booth. No one is seated at the counter. Mike and Cal take the booth at the opposite end of the diner. The midnight diner shift consists of a short order cook and a waitress, who shuffles up beside the men from across the low barrier.

"What'll you boys have?" she asks, looking at them over her black horn-rimmed glasses, pin in hand.

"Coffee, sweetheart." Cal grins at her. "And bring me that two egg special I saw on the board as I came in."

"How about you, hon?"

"That sounds good. The same."

"How you like your eggs?"

"Scrambled," Cal answers.

"Over light," Mike orders. "But make mine with hash browns instead of grits."

She brings the men coffee—hot, dark, and steaming. Cal drinks his as it is. Mike doctors his with cream and sugar.

"You're ruining a great cup of coffee, Snake," Cal observes.

"I like a little coffee with my cream and sugar."

"I like my coffee like I like my women—hot and black." Cal laughs.

"I call bullshit on that." Mike grins back. "I've seen your lovely wife."

"Yeah, it is. And she is lovely. Thanks for noticing. It sure sounds funny, though."

"So I hear you're headed to the longwall," Mike says, stirring his coffee and adding cream until the mixture is a golden brown.

"Yep. Old man told me the other day. Me and Jeff Rose are going over to Gary and look at their set up in a few weeks. I hear this machine is something to see. Mines more coal in an hour that a conventional miner can in a shift." Cal takes a long swig off his cup. "Kinda surprised you ain't goin' with us."

"Wasn't invited."

"Old man never mentioned it to ya?"

"Not once."

"You piss him off?" Cal asks, looking over the rim of his coffee cup.

"Don't know. Reckon I don't have my suction up as much as you do," Mike chides.

"Fuck you," Cal retorts. "Think your thing with the old man's daughter had anything to do with it?"

Mike looks at Cal. He's never said a word to anyone, anywhere, at any time, to any of the bosses about Jennifer, but he knows there are no secrets in the coal mine.

He sighs. "Hell, who knows? I ain't lost any sleep over being passed over. I mean, he picked good men. More than that, though, I ain't sure I want to commit to something like that anyway. To be honest, I don't know how much longer I'm going to be here, Cal."

The waitress brings their orders and the men dig in.

"Whatta ya mean by that, young'un?" Cal asks as he shovels the eggs into his mouth.

"Don't know right yet, old man," Mike kids. "Been thinking about trying my hand at something else."

"Like what? What else you gonna do 'round here? In these hills, you ain't got a lot of options. You're a coal miner, or do something that services the miners and the mines. You know, a doctor, a lawyer, or an Injun chief." Cal grins. "Those are the only jobs around here. I know you got your paper now, but you ain't no doctor or lawyer. You damn sure ain't no injun chief. You could be a teacher, but that job sure don't pay much. Hell, we got former teachers workin' in the hole with us now."

"Sounds like you pretty much got it pegged, Cal. I said pretty much the same thing recently. Can't argue with you there. But I've been thinking a lot about the mines since Wildcat checked out. And you're right, the money's good. That's what's seductive about it. You're making good money, and you get used to it. You buy a nice car, then a house, then kids come along. Before you know it, you've spent a lifetime in the hole, and you're broke down and you've got black lung and you're looking for that doctor and that lawyer. I don't want that for me, and I damn sure don't want that to be my legacy for my kids—if I ever have any."

Cal puts his fork down. "It's been good enough for your paw. It's been a good life for me."

"And that's great for you. Look, I ain't knocking it. It's honest work, and there's good folks working down there. It's just that I want something else, Cal. For me. You see, buddy, I don't wanna live for work. And that's what my dad's done his entire life. Get up, eat, go to work, sleep. We work for money, and we all think that's what's important. I mean, you can't live without money, but that's not what's important."

Cal shakes his head and laughs. "OK, Snake, you're out there. If money ain't important, then tell me what is."

"Time, Cal. Time is what's important. We all think we've got all the time in the world, but we don't. Like I've always heard about the guy on his deathbed never saying he wished he'd spent more time at work, well, I don't wanna look back in thirty years and the only thing I see is this deep dark hole."

Cal stares dumbfounded at the young man. "Hell, I ain't never thought about nothing like that. I just wanna do my job and be left the hell alone. Boy, you make my head hurt. If college makes you think about shit like this, I'm glad I never finished high school."

The waitress brings the bill. "I've got this," Mike picks up the tab.

"Well, thank'y kindly, young man. Least you could do after making me listen to all this bullshit." Cal smiles good-naturedly at the man.

"Reckon so. Didn't mean to overload that pea-brain of yours," Mike kids back.

"No problem. We'll do it again anytime, as long as you're buying."

Cal is quiet on the drive back to the mine, as if processing all Mike has said. He opens the door to exit the car, then turns and looks at Mike.

"We're all just trying to get through this life as best we can, Mike. Every man has to make his own way and find his own peace. I hope you can find yours, my buddy." He half-smiles at him, then disappears into the darkness.

Chapter 36

Mr. Dwight Cone, Superintendent
Banner Fuels Corp
Welch, WV

Dear Mr. Cone:
This letter will inform you of my intention to leave
my supervisory position following the completion of my
shift two weeks from the date of this letter. I am
Sincerely,
Michael Thomas

That's it, Mike thinks. He learned in one of his college classes that business letters should be short, direct, and succinct. This letter accomplishes those objectives. Since it's his first actual business letter, he wanted it to be proper.

He drives out to the main office and drops the letter off at the super's office after his shift. The secretary takes the letter and, without reading, it places it on the super's desk. He feels relieved. His decision is made, and now he's gotta get packing.

The shift the following day goes smoothly. The crew knows nothing of his decision, and Mike will tell them once the higher ups decide what they will do. After completing his paperwork, as Mike heads to the showers, the old man thunders at him from his office.

"Thomas, get your ass in here NOW!"

Mike stops dead in his tracks. He knows what it's about, and he lets out a heavy sigh. He enters the old man's office.

"What the hell is this?" Theodore demands, grasping the resignation letter tight in his hand, shaking it at the young man.

"It's what it says it is. My notice."

"So you're leaving here. Why?"

"I just want to do something else."

"Now what kind of fucking bullshit is that? What the hell else are you gonna do?"

"Don't know. I'll figure it out later."

The old man shakes his head. "I swear, for the life of me, I don't understand you young people. So you gonna go off somewhere and 'find yourself'?" The old man makes quotation marks in the air with his hands. "I thought that went out a while back."

The old man's gestures surprise Mike. He's never seen the old man act this way. He's seen him mad as hell, even violent at times, but never sarcastic.

"Well, I don't know about that. But I do know I wanna try my hand at something above ground."

"What the hell else is there to do around here except coal mining, son? That's what we do 'round here."

"I know that. I don't plan on staying round here."

"Got your degree and getting the hell out, huh?"

"Something like that."

The old man continues shaking his head. "I don't get you, Thomas. I've known you since you were a small boy sucking at your mama's tit. Watched you grow up, went to your games in high school. Always thought you were a good kid. Never figured you for a quitter."

The words hit Mike hard. He struggles to remain calm. "I don't see it like that, sir. I see it as a choice. I'm gonna try something out of the coal mines and away from here."

"I, I, I. Me, me, me. Always thinking about yourself. There are other folks affected by your decision."

"This place will get along fine without me."

"Oh, no doubt. This place goes on no matter what. I can replace you in a New York minute."

"So, then, what's the problem?"

"I just wanted you to know how disappointed I am with your 'choice.'" He again makes the air quotes. "How disappointed I am with you. You were beginning to make a fair section boss. You were starting to do me a good job and now you're quitting. You quit on Jennifer first. Now you're quitting on me." The old man never looks up at Mike.

Mike stands almost at attention. The old man's words cut to his core. "Am I fired?" he asks.

The old man finally looks up and glares at Mike. "No. You did the proper thing and gave notice. Lord knows I've had men who never said nothing. Just didn't show up one day and never came back. Work out your notice. I'll get your replacement lined up, and he can spend the last week with you and your crew."

Mike nods, turns, and leaves the office without saying anything to the old man. He has plenty to say, but keeps his words to himself. Whatever he offered wouldn't make a difference to the old man. His mentor's mind is made up, and for that, Mike has regret. The old man has been good to him. Like a father almost. It's ironically funny: he disappointed his father taking a company job, and now he's disappointed the only other man whose opinion ever mattered to him.

Life is pain. There is the pain of birth and growing up, of being shunned in school, of being rejected by a crush. There is pain in discipline, the discipline he has endured going to school and working in the deep, dark, wet, dirty, and dangerous mines every day. And there is pain in disappointment. Walking toward the bathhouse, Mike realizes the pain of disappointment is worse than the pain of discipline. It really is time to leave.

Chapter 37

Mike doesn't know what to expect this last day. Everything outside the mine is completed. He's sold off all his possessions, given up the apartment. He gave his once-shiny new Mickey Mouse touch tone telephone to his little sister. He can see her gabbing incessantly on the phone like all teenagers do. The car is loaded, and as soon as his shift is done, he's rolling out. He hasn't seen Jennifer in the months since their last meeting, and perhaps, it's just as well. Not really anything left to be said between them. Same with her father. Dressing in the foreman's bath house this morning, little is said. Everyone knows it is his last day, and he's made it clear over the last two weeks that he'd prefer no one makes too big a deal out of his leaving. Except Jeff Rose. He walks up and gives Mike a rib-crushing bear hug.

"Headin' out, boss?"

"Reckon so."

"Damn sure hate to see ya go. Say, you wouldn't wanna sell your hard hat, would ya? I'll give ya a couple hundred dollars for it."

Mike shakes his head. "Damn fair offer, Jeff, but no. Reckon I'll keep it as a souvenir of my time here."

"Ah, hell. Thought I'd ask anyway. Hold it in the road, Snake."

Cal Ripley comes over and sits beside Mike on the bench. The two exchange a short look. Cal grins at him.

"So, this is it, huh? Sure you gonna do this?" he asks.

"Oh, yeah. It's time, man. Past time for me."

"I hate it, Snake. I really do. I had hoped you'd hang around and we'd be running this place someday."

Mike gives him a little shrug. "Appreciate the thought, Cal. Have to admit there was a time a few years back when I might've thought like you do. But over time, I've come to realize I want more out of life than this. This place ain't me."

"Man's gotta do something."

"Oh, yeah. I get that. But I want to do more than this. This is my dad's life. This is Theodore's life. Up to now it's been my life. I don't want it to be my life anymore."

"Damn, that's deep. You think too much." Cal smiles. "So what are you gonna do?"

"You know what? I ain't got no plans. Got no family to worry about. Got some money saved up that will last me a little while. I'm going to the beach for a week or two, stick my feet in the ocean. I really liked it there. After that, I don't know. I'd like to teach. Maybe coach. Like you said, a man's gotta do something."

"You'll be back. This place is in your blood." Cal loads his jaw with chewing tobacco.

"Nope. I've spent my last shift in these holes."

"If there's one thing I've learned in life, it's never say never." Cal spits into the drain in the floor. "You never know what the future holds."

"Reckon that's true." Mike nods. "Well, then let's say I ain't got no plans on returning."

"Fair enough," Cal says, then looks over at the young man. "Look, I don't know how you left it with the old man . . ."

"Not well, I think."

"Anyway, know that there will always be a place for you here. I can promise you that." He rises and extends his hand.

"Thanks for that, Cal."

"You will be missed."

"Now that's bullshit. This place is bigger than any one of us. The place won't even miss a beat."

"Reckon that's true for any of us. Anyhow, hold it in the road." The men shake and Cal leaves the bathhouse. Mike finishes putting on his dirty work clothes and walks outside. His replacement has already scoped the workmen, and all are present for this shift. Mike looks around the yard at the workmen milling around awaiting the cage. The workers are adjusting their lamps, drinking a cup of coffee, or taking the last drags off their cigarettes, quiet as is the usual case early in the mountain morning. Mike studies the workmen. Most are young men, like him, but look much older than their years. Coal mining is a young man's game, and it sucks the life out of you. *If I stay, I die a slow death, either from black lung or broken down from injury or dragged down from the continual beating of the mine.* This is a tough way to make a living, and the mine always wins. How many lives has the mine claimed over the years? Either directly, like Polecat and Stinky, or indirectly, like Wildcat? A man shouldn't have to put his life on the line to feed his family, yet these folks do every day, and never complain. It is their lot in life. *It doesn't have to be mine,* he believes.

The crew goes through their daily routine. Their new boss efficiently oversees what is now his crew, leaving Mike to hang out his last shift in the dinner hole. The crew does take a last lunch together, and the crew has brought a nice white cake with white icing, Mike's favorite, for lunch. The crew kids Mike incessantly during their lunch.

"You'll be back. You'll miss this place," Lou says simply.

"Hell, he's just taking an extended vacation. If I was him, with all his money, I'd take a couple of months off if I could too!" Larry adds, stuffing cake into his pie hole.

"Once he sobers up, he'll come back. The money is just too good," Randy tosses in. "Where the hell else is a man gonna make this kinda money?"

"Why, hell yeah," Dave chimes in. "He'll be back, tanned and rested and ready for more. Only the old man will sentence him to owl shift next time!" Which brings a chortle from every one.

All seem to enjoy picking at him. All except Kate. She is usually quiet, but today says even less. The ride out is uneventful, and as the cage empties at shift's end, the workers scatter. There are no long good-byes, just the way Mike wanted it. Mike washes the mud from his work boots, and turning off the water, he looks up to see Kate standing, staring at him. She walks over, takes off her hard hat, and lets her long red hair fall over her shoulders. Even the black coal dust cannot hide her beauty.

"So this is good-bye I reckon?" he asks.

"You never know what the future holds, Mike Thomas. Go put that degree to work for ya. You earned it. But don't forget us." She smiles at him, her eyes welling up. "Don't forget me." She looks down at the ground.

"I'll try hard to forget this place," he says to her. Then, raising her face with his finger, looks into her green eyes. "But I can guarantee I will never, ever forget you." He wants to kiss her, but this is not the place. He's leaving, but she'll still be here, and she doesn't need the tongues wagging about her. It's hard enough on women in this world without giving these hard asses anything extra.

"Where you heading?" Her question is more than a simple question, almost as if there is a "do you want some company?" buried in there with it.

"You know," he half-laughs, "I ain't got a stinking clue. South. A place where the sun comes up bright in the morning and stays high in the sky all day. I've lived most of my life in the cold and wet and dark. Reckon I'll go somewhere that's not like that. Get a job where I can see the day."

"Well, that sounds good." She smiles. "Work on your tan some. You're way too pale." He realizes he'll miss her barbs.

"Can do. I'll write you. You can send me some suntan lotion."

"I'll send you more than that," she teases. "See you 'round, Mike Thomas," and Kate disappears into the female bathhouse, giving him a long glance over her shoulder as the door closes. Mike enters the foreman's bathhouse ahead of the other foremen, who are still completing their paperwork. He tosses his hard hat across the floor and watches it spin to a stop against the opposite wall. He picks it up and places it into his green duffle bag, along with his mine belt. His bank clothes he throws into the trash. He showers quickly, wanting to make his escape before the rest of the foremen make their way in. He leaves in a sprint, throwing his duffle into the trunk of the Mustang and slowly eases the car out of the lot and onto the narrow highway. He cruises down the road, past his childhood home and through the dirty streets of Welch and onto Highway 52 toward Bluefield, driving the road he'd driven hundreds of times before, only this time without any hurry. He steers the car onto Interstate 77 South, through the East River Mountain tunnel, leaving West Virginia in his rearview mirror and drives leisurely into the Virginia night.

Epilogue

Three years later . . .

Bottom of the ninth. Score tied at two. Two out. Runner on third. The skinny second baseman has just taken a high fastball outside to even the count at one and one, steps out of the box and stares down his third base coach for the sign.

Mike studies the situation. His batter is not a strong hitter, which is why he's hitting in this spot in the order. His runner on third, the center fielder, is the fastest runner on the squad. His ball club has already made it farther in the playoffs than anyone expected, and if they can pull this out, it would make the first time the Gulfport High School Admirals had made it to the regionals in ten years. What the hell. Let's go for it.

Mike goes through a series of meaningless gestures then touches the bill of his ball cap. The indicator. The next sign was the actual instruction to his batter. He dusts off the trouser legs of his uniform.

Safety squeeze.

The batter nods and steps into the box. The tall, lanky left hander has been firing his fastball effectively all day and isn't worried about the runner stealing home. The third baseman is playing back, allowing the runner to take a larger-than-normal lead from third. The pitcher gives the runner a quick glance then delivers to home.

The ball is dead down the middle, and the little man lays down a picture-perfect drag bunt down the third base line. The runner does as he should, waiting to break until the batter puts the ball on the ground, then sprinting wildly down the baseline toward the plate. The ball rolls slowly past him as the pitcher and third baseman collapse on the ball. The catcher crouches in front of the plate, screaming madly for the throw. The runner slides across the plate well before the tag.

The dugout empties, hats and gloves flying wildly, and a scrum ensues at home plate. Mike stands in the coach's box watching the melee, then turns and looks into the stands.

Kate Matthews Thomas holds their newborn daughter in her arms, smiling proudly at her husband.

Afterword

A remarkable author once said, "Most people die with their story still inside them."

This novel is my story, out before I die.

When discussing this project with my family, my son told me I was probably the only person on earth who could tell this story. I wouldn't begin to say that, but I do feel it is not just my story.

It is the story of a way of life no longer there, of a people who no longer exist, save for scattered pockets up myriad hollers in the Appalachians. Of a hard-working, hard-living group who took their lives in their hands every day to feed their families. It was the only way of life most of them ever knew. I was fortunate enough to escape. Many didn't. Those that didn't had their way of life taken from them by the government, through stifling environmental regulations that made it cost-prohibitive to mine coal. The miners once lamented that the coal operators took the coal out of southern West Virginia and left nothing for the workers. Not true. They were paid. Now, the government has taken those jobs from them and truly left them with nothing. No prospects for a better life on the horizon, many have turned to prescription drugs or methamphetamine. Illicit drug use is rampant in what were once the coal fields. Even if the coal jobs returned, it's not for certain there would be enough able bodies to fill them.

This story is of a time long gone, of a proud and hard-working people. Like most of life's occurrences with the passage of time, I remember it fondly. I hope this novel gave you a glimpse into that time.

It is often said writing is a solitary act. I won't debate that point here, but what I will note is once the writing is complete, it takes a bunch of folks to turn that working manuscript into something fit for public consumption. Thanks to my daughter Lauren for her expert editing, publishing advice, and being my number one cheerleader. Now there are two published authors in the family! Thanks to my son Kevyn for coming up with this title and convincing me this title was better than the initial one. He was right. I have no doubt this project would not have seen the light of day without my children's support. Thanks to Donna Riordan for her insight and advice. Your eyes made the project better. A book editor is born! And finally, thanks to my wife, Karen. Everything I am and ever will be is because all those years ago she saw something in a broken-down coal miner he did not see in himself. How do you repay someone for that? This novel is for her.

About the Author

Ernie Bowling was born in the coalfields of Eastern Kentucky and spent his formative years in the West Virginia coal towns of Mullens and Welch. A third-generation coal miner, he received an associate of science degree in mining engineering technology from Bluefield State College. He spent ten years working in coal mines in West Virginia and Alabama before returning to college. Ernie received his bachelor of science, master of science, and doctor of optometry degrees from the University of Alabama at Birmingham. He spent a year in residence with an ophthalmologist in Bluefield, West Virginia, returning south when he purchased his first optometric practice. Ernie has served as associate professor and head of the primary care service at the UAB School of Optometry and is currently in private practice in Gadsden, Alabama. He is a fellow and a diplomate of the American Academy of Optometry, a fellow of the American College of Medical Optometry, and a distinguished practitioner and fellow of the prestigious National Academies of Practice. A prolific author and international speaker, Ernie was the chief optometric editor of *Optometry Times*, one of optometry's leading trade journals. Ernie is a past recipient of the Georgia Optometric Associations Bernard Kahn Memorial Award for outstanding service to the optometric profession and a past recipient of the Energeyes Associations Presidents Council Award. *Coal Blooded* is his first novel. He invites you to check out his website erniebowling.com. Contact Ernie by e-mail at erniebowling@icloud.com and follow him on Twitter: @erniebowling.

CPSIA information can be obtained
at www.ICGtesting.com
Printed in the USA
LVOW11s0459010218
564856LV00001B/13/P